Remembering Hell

By

Helen Downing

Louise Patterson is back! Now a long-term resident of Heaven, Louise finds a need to return to the one place she thought she had left behind forever – HELL. Back in Central City Hades, she meets Joe who needs a guardian angel. Louise also meets a tall, dark and handsome stranger who just may change her afterlife. In this compelling sequel to 'Awake In Hell', you are invited to return to the land of the damned with Louise as she learns a whole new set of lessons about how to live a good life, even after you're dead.

For:
My loving husband, Larry
Always...

ACKNOWLEDGEMENTS

Larry – for your understanding through this whole process. You have to know agape if you are going to be married to a writer! I will love you in life and beyond.
Gabrielle – you are a great photographer and a great friend.
Linda and Patch – for being great kids. I love you!
Mom – for passing on the "writing gene," and for giving me the best role model anyone could have.
Dad – for giving me a foundation on which to build my faith, and for allowing me to take my own path.
Michelle and Diana – for being those friends who understand they have to share me with my imaginary friends.
Every single reader – for giving me a chance.

CHAPTER ONE

The old woman wakes up suddenly, startled perhaps by continued life itself, with no idea where she is. Then it dawns on her. She's in her recliner in the living room. *Damn*, she thinks to herself, *I fell asleep in front of the TV again*. She gingerly starts to shift in the roomy seat as if lubricating her old bones in preparation of getting up. *Getting old isn't for pussies.* She laughs out loud at her own joke. She starts to rise, sits down hard, and tries again. After the second false start she almost regrets not allowing her niece to buy her that electric recliner with the automatic seat that will dump a person out like a giant regurgitating monster at the push of a button.

When she's finally upright, she glances at the television to check the time. Her life has become so predictable that a glance is all it takes. There is no clock on the TV, but she can estimate the time based on what is on, and what is happening on the program. She has become quite the creature of habit in her advanced age, and despite the fact there is little to no chance that will ever change, it doesn't stop her from hating herself for it.

According to undeniable evidence—first round of Jeopardy—it is around seven-fifteen in the evening. That doesn't give her much time. Her husband will be home within the half hour after his hard day of hanging out with a bunch of other old coots at the lodge shooting the shit all day. To say she's amazed by the fact that the same half-dozen geezers can consistently show up to the same place every day and still have anything at all to talk about is an understatement. Not that they need new material. The old favorites: The world is going to hell in a handbasket, what happened to music/movies/sports teams,

9

what those kids today are thinking with the way they dress/behave/think/act is standard fare for her other half and his cronies. If they had their way, John Wayne would still be riding tall, President Reagan would have been elected King of America, and Clint Eastwood would have remained a badass before he got old and turned into a wuss making chick flicks that make folks cry. What happens to men when they get old? Why do every single one of them turn into Grandpa from the Waltons?

She is smiling to herself as she ambles into the kitchen. When you are young, you never think about the end. Sure, when she was a girl she would imagine growing old with her friends and her husband, but that was more about growing up, not growing old. The fact is, you don't think about it because to contemplate aging means facing the fact that you are going to die. And while every human being spends some time reflecting on how or when they will meet their personal demise, we spend no time imagining what it will be like to wake up in a body that doesn't work anymore, or to look at a reflection of a decrepit version of what we once were. Death is a stealthy creature for most of us. It sneaks up behind us while we aren't paying attention, then all of a sudden you know deep within you, that the world has left you behind. And for her, that is not metaphorical. Sometimes she feels as though she's the last real person at the party.

Once again she wonders why she's been chosen from all those she's known and loved to be cursed with damnable longevity. There were those, some of whom she can hardly bear to think about let alone name, who led incredible lives. Some had families, some had adventures, and one had it all. In the meantime, she's lived small and unimportant. But she's lived long.

She reaches into the cabinet underneath the counter for a large pot. Then almost by rote she begins to reach up into cupboards for spices and into the freezer for meat and tomato sauce, then one more stop under the sink and she's ready to begin. As she's rising from her last trip around the kitchen, her eyes fall on the now dead flowers her husband had presented her the previous week for her eighty-ninth birthday. She laughs quietly as she scoops them out of the vase and into the trash. *This is what I get for living almost a century,* she thinks ruefully. *More things that decay and die before I do.* Exactly a week ago her husband had come in with them, at the time in full bloom and color, in a huge bouquet wrapped with a large red bow. It's not that she hates flowers, but she doesn't exactly love them either. She ended up feeling as ambiguous about her gift as she did about her actual birthday. And lately about her life.

The microwave starts beeping so she goes over and gets the Tupperware container now filled with sauce in place of the block of red ice she has put inside. She pours it in the pot while the burger is browning in a frying pan on the burner next to it. She lets out a long tired moan as she lifts the heavy pan and dumps the meat into the pot. Then she begins to stir and get lost in thought. She remembers a saying. 'If I had any decency I would be dead. Everyone else is.' That thought brings another laugh to the surface. Who had said that? It was someone famous. That terrible woman from the Algonquin Round Table. What was her name?

Memory is of course a luxury for the young. After eighty-nine years, the old woman can barely even remember those people who have left her long ago. She also can't remember falling in love, or the feeling of the first kiss, or anything that felt really good. She can't remember doing anything great, and she can't remember doing anything really bad either. She is as ordinary as the sauce she's making. No one ever complains about spaghetti for dinner, but no food critics ever review it either.

She had only married once, believe it or not. In this day and age, everyone takes a mulligan on the marriage thing. If they even marry at all. She had not been too young, but it wasn't desperation either. She could have hung on for a few more years for something better, but she didn't. She seems to remember that she loved him. They had never had children. It wasn't by choice, but it didn't tear them apart like some couples. They always felt if it was meant to be, then kids would come. And kids came. Other people's kids. Her niece is her favorite. With that face that reminds her of a long gone sister whom she's loved with all her heart. She convinced everyone that she had no biological clock nor any facsimile of one. She constantly referred to her life as "carefree and unhindered," and talked about how she could go anywhere at the drop of a hat or do anything on a whim. No one ever had the nerve to mention that she had gone nowhere and done nothing. She imagined they believed she was internally wrecked by the fact that she was barren. Likewise, she never had the nerve to tell them that she wasn't bothered at all.

She continues to stir with one hand while reaching blindly with the other and begins adding spices without even a glance. She doesn't have to measure anymore. She has made this exact dish every Wednesday for the last fifty-eight years. That was her husband. A Monday is meatloaf, Friday is Chinese take-out, and Wednesday is spaghetti kind of man. He was kind but not loving. He was decent but never righteous. He never raised his voice or hand to her, but he also never went out of his way to compliment her. He had gone to work every single day for almost forty years, yet never displayed any ambition. He was a good man with no passion, and that made her sad.

In the beginning they had made love often. But then it just dwindled from twice a week to Saturday nights to on birthdays and anniversaries to never. They had never had an actual conversation about sex in all the years they were having it, and neither one of them seemed to miss it terribly once it was gone.

The one thing she does remember is the first day that she realized she was old. Really old. She woke up and looked in the mirror and saw an old woman peering back at her. Watery light eyes, translucent skin barely stretched over creaky bones. She started to cry as she realized her life was now behind her. She had gotten a seat at the table, and she had been satisfied with meatloaf and spaghetti. Now, every course had been served and all that was left was to wait for the bill to arrive.

These days she is used to the idea. In fact, she's getting a little impatient. She has served her time, now isn't she supposed to go on? Move to the next plane, come back as a housecat, whatever is supposed to happen? Can't it just happen already? Then she realizes there's something heavy in her hand. She looks down and to her surprise she is adding a new ingredient to her sauce. "How funny," she says quizzically as she continues to pour.

After she has administered half the box into the pot, she replaces the Rat-B-Gone under the sink.

She hears the front door open and close. "Honey, I'm home!" her husband yells.

"Dorothy Parker!" she exclaims as he walks into the kitchen.

"No, try again," he says dryly as he sits down at the table.

"Sorry, I just remembered the name of a woman who said something important," she says as she makes a heaping helping of spaghetti and sets it down in front of him, just as he lifts his fork. It's a dance they've been doing for almost sixty years. He asks about her day before he fills his mouth with a giant bite. She begins to ramble about the neighbors getting new puppies, shih tzus she thinks, and so that woman who wears heels even to the grocery store has had to walk them at least four times. "It's a wonder she doesn't have bunions the size of oranges!" she says as she begins to rinse off the utensils and run hot water in the frying pan she used to cook her deadly meal.

Within fifteen minutes she hears his labored breathing. She turns her back to him and starts wiping the counters. "I also found some adorable sweaters at Walmart," she goes on, as if nothing unusual is happening. "I thought we could pick a few up and put them in the Christmas closet for the girls." She winces slightly as he crashes to the floor, turning over the chair with him. He's convulsing and a weird foamy mixture of sauce and bile is coming from his mouth. Finally, he stops seizing and she moves back to the stove. "Now go on, and don't worry. You'll do fine in Heaven," she says as she sets her own plate on the table across from his now limp body.

She picks up her phone from the counter and dials 911. When the operator answers she calmly gives their address and tells the woman on the other end that there are two people dead inside. Then she hangs up and begins to eat. Her last thought is one of comfort, because if he is going to Heaven, then she won't have to face him after this horrible deed. She says to no one in particular, "I have a feeling I will be going somewhere else."

CHAPTER TWO

"Fuck, fuck, fuckity, fuck!!"

The words just fly out of my mouth. It's like only yesterday I was a cabbie in Hell and filling the boss's "curse jar" took up the majority of my disposable income. However, that is not the case. I have called Heaven my address for a great many years.

My name is Louise Patterson, and I died and went to Hell. Whether or not I deserved it, or if I did indeed earned the redemption that I finally found are purely subjective. However, I did end up here, in Paradise where everything is cool and folks are happy and the general population tends to frown upon the gratuitous use of the F bomb.

"Lou! Haven't heard you talk like a truck driver since…well, since you were a truck driver!" Will says, laughing at his own joke. Will is one of my dearest friends up here. At one time, he was my guardian angel. I was once damned to eternal temp jobs, and Will had to stalk me. He was so bad at it I almost always saw him hiding or following me. Good times. Well, not really, but I've learned to remember the good and let go of the bad.

I get up from the wall of screens I've been parked in front of for the past few hours. We are in the central office at WF&PI. The "company," as we call it, is a remote viewing center for family members and curious angels to look in on what is happening on Earth. This is a wondrous place, and if people watching is a hobby of yours in life? You'll want to spend a great deal of time here once you are dead. Joyous occasions are celebrated tenfold up here, with generations of families reuniting for weddings or births or even deaths. When someone shuffles off the mortal coil, they are brought here where they can be welcomed back into the bosom of love from everyone who knew them in life. That is, as long as they make it here. If they end up in the opposite place, they are usually alone and confused for a while. But it doesn't take long to figure it out. For me, I knew I was in Hell the second I realized that I had no choice in what I could wear every day, and the supernatural closet that was providing my outfits had been programmed by someone for which torment and disgrace came as naturally as mother's milk to a newborn. At the time I thought it was some kind of Devil. In reality, the one person who knows how to punish someone more acutely than anyone else is one's self.

When I got to Heaven and could choose my occupation I considered working here. In the end my ambition got the better of me, and I chose a different path. But I like to spend my extra time here. I get to see my parents or grandparents occasionally when they come in to hang out and watch my daughter or grandchildren or great-grandchildren.

It's bizarre to think of myself as a great-grandmother since my appearance hasn't changed since my demise. I died of breast cancer when I was forty-five years old. That means I get to be middle-aged for eternity. Lucky me! I watch from on high as my family and friends go on with life. Many of them aged and eventually passed and came here. I try not to take it personally when a few of them look at me with surprise, as though I was the last person they'd expect to see in Heaven. But most of the ones I was closest to were very happy to see me. Almost as happy as I was to see them. There is a great sense of peace when someone I love shows up here. I get to be part of the welcoming, with smiles and tears and eternal agape. Agape is my favorite word. It means unconditional love. And I've been fortunate, that all of my loved ones who died ended up here immediately. No one had to take the detour I did through Hell before finding their place in eternal bliss.

Well, at least not yet.

Will is now studying me with sincere concern. "Maybe I should call ahead to the agency and warn them that you're coming," he says, tapping his Bluetooth earpiece.

"Not necessary," I say quickly as I walk to the elevator and punch the down button. "Gabby is at the front desk. She's already briefing Deedy."

"How do you know?" Will asks with wonder.

"No, I haven't sprouted any remote viewing power or anything," I say, half joking and half resentfully. "I just know Gabby. And I feel it in my bones." "You know your bones aren't real, right?" Will says with a smile.

"Yeah? But I bet if I hit you in your imaginary nose bone it'll hurt!" I tease.

The doors open, and I'm on the elevator. "And don't bother trying to follow me. I doubt you've gotten any better at it in the last quarter-century or so…" I say as the doors close. Will is wagging his finger at me, like a father to a toddler who's just sassed at him. I just give him my most alluring smile as the doors shut.

As I start down the long trip back to the street and down the few blocks to the agency, I think about Gabby. Gabby is short for Gabrielle, and she is an archangel. Yeah, the one you're thinking of. Don't worry, I thought it was a man too. Anyway, Gabby as part of the "top dogs" of the Angelic hierarchy comes complete with glorious wings and a set of superpowers that would make Stan Lee jealous enough to cry. One of those superpowers is that she can read minds. Well, kind of. What I've learned over the years is that she can't exactly read minds.

It is more like she can hear what is in your heart or soul or whatever. Of course, a lot of times, it seems that she is answering a question that you have just formulated in your mind, hence the mind reader rap.

But have you ever noticed that a lot of questions that we as humans think about are actually things we've been aware of on some level for a very long time? I heard once that slot machines in casinos are constantly putting together combinations. The second you put in a coin and pull the lever, it lands on whatever combination the machine had already decided on at that very second. Our inner voice speaks to us all the time too, and it is only when we land on a particular thought that it is able to enter our minds, where we can process it. Gabby can tell you that your soul is going to come up with three cherries or two lemons and an orange, so to speak. At any rate, she's totally brilliant. I vacillate between being completely in love with her and being outrageously envious of her at the same time.

However, as I walk into the agency and see the way Gabby is looking at me, I realize I am also quite frightened of her. Her face is filled with something not quite angry, but there is a fire within her eyes that alludes to angelic fury. Now before you start thinking that angelic fury is on par with angry puppies or spitting mad adorable babies, let me remind you that angelic fury was once responsible for things like killing the first born of entire countries and shit like that. When Gabby gets mad, or to better describe it, righteously infuriated, particularly on Deedy's behalf, then she gets scary. And not like when you were a kid and your mom said "Wait until your father gets home!" kind of scary. I'm talking Chuck Norris would shit his pants kind of scary. So a ticked off angel is not on the top ten "must see" list in the hereafter. And while I've never actually seen Gabby's wrath, I have heard enough stories to know I don't want to. Ever.

"Okay, I know you're pissed off at me right now. But no smiting me or anything," I say with a false bravado and accompany it with a nervous giggle. I walk past her to the coffee pot. "May I have a cup of your wonderful coffee?" I'm trying to sound way more nonchalant than I actually feel.

"I'm not angry, Lou. And of course, but please let me get it. Whenever you get near my coffee you always make a huge mess," she says with genuine laughter. Thankfully, she's in a good mood.

I laugh along with her. "When I was living, Bobby used to call my sugar packets and dirty spoons Weasel Scat." When I was in Hell, I couldn't even remember Bobby. It took years and a little of Deedy's magic before I remembered I had shared my life with a wonderful man. A wonderful man who called me Weasel, but still a great guy. Now, of course he is here, in Heaven. Along with his wife, a wonderful woman named Sue Ann who he married a few years after I died. The two of them raised my daughter, Dinny. Dinny was a nickname too. Bobby loved nicknames. Her actual name was Linda, after my best friend in the whole world.

Thinking about Linda snaps me back into the present, and I decide I am willing to push the edge of the envelope with Gabby. "You know why I'm here, Gabby. I need to talk to the boss." I decide that perhaps being a bit more respectful might be required here, so I quickly add, "If that's okay?"

"That is always okay, Louise," Gabby answers with a small smile. "But you aren't just asking to talk to him, you are quite frankly demanding that he comes and talks to you." She hands me my coffee. "You don't think that might be just a bit presumptuous?"

"Why?" I say with total sincerity. I breathe in the

aroma of the coffee before taking the first sip.

Gabby gives me the kind of smile you give to a child who just asked why the sky is blue. "Because you are basically asking for a command performance from the Boss for something you already know how is going to end, sweetie."

My eyes start to fill, and I clear my throat before I begin to speak. "I'm sorry, I really am," I say, and I mean it. "I know I'm acting like a spoiled brat, but this is a hill I'm willing to die on," I continue. "You know, if I could…die again." I half-heartedly laugh at my own joke.

Gabby opens her arms and brings me in to her for a warm embrace. While I am enjoying the contact, as well as the natural healing power of her touch, she looks down at me with an expression that is so sweet there are no words to describe it in a way that anyone living would ever understand. There are some breathtakingly beautiful moments you will just have to wait until the afterlife to comprehend.

Then the air changes, and I can feel the excitement. I look up at Gabby and see the sparkle in her eyes that I know is reflected in mine too. "The Boss is here," she says.

Suddenly his booming voice fills the corridor. "Gabby, if you don't mind, could you ask Ms. Patterson to come in here before her poor head explodes?" His humor is evident.

The sound of Deedy's voice, rolling in with that heavy Welsh accent is always soothing to me, no matter how jangled my nerves may be. Intellectually, I know that he's not always Welsh, not always dressed to the nines in the finest suits, not always called Mr. Deedy, not even always a "he" for that matter. But to me, he is now, and will eternally be Mr. Deedy, because for whatever reason, that is what I need him to be. For others he may be older, or younger, or black, or blue, or female. He can create himself to look like anything, because after all, he created everything and everyone.

Yes. It's true. I get to see God as a six feet five inches skinny dude with a funny accent and a great wardrobe.

I practically sprint down the hall to Deedy's office. I pause at the door as usual to reflect the first time I ever came here and stood in front of this door. The first time I ever walked through it, I was a resident of Hell. Convinced that I deserved an eternity of suffering, I came here to work for a strange, enigmatic man who, as far as I knew, owned a temp agency. But this office was the birthplace of my redemption. This place was where I realized I was forgiven, and it was here where I discovered I had actually been doing temp jobs for God.

I walk in like a woman with purpose and start talking even before I take my usual seat across from his huge desk. "Okay, so I know you already know why I'm here, and I have been thinking about this ever since it happened," I say, my speech already prepared in my head so I could just lay out my argument with at least a bit of eloquence. "I know she did something horrific, and I heard her last words, which basically was her giving herself her own trial and judgment. But her life as a whole—" I cannot finish because Deedy interrupts me.

"Hello, Louise!" Deedy says casually, as though I haven't said a word yet. He addresses me like two old friends running into each other on the street. "How long has it been? A few years since we have been face to face? Although, I must admit, I really do love our evening chats," he says with a sly smile.

I look at him with exasperation. I did not pray until after I was dead. Is that weird? But since I'd never done it before, except to kind of fake it when I was a kid in church, I reverted back to my only research which were movies and television from my childhood. I started praying every night before bed, on my knees with my fingers interlocked and my elbows on the mattress. At first I felt silly, like I was talking to myself, but since I knew for a fact that there was a God, I just talked to Deedy, exactly the way I would talk to him if I was sitting directly across from him. I feel something very much like gratitude to know he is actually listening when I pray. However, I am also starting to feel pissed off that now that I'm right in front of him he has decided to deliberately not listen.

"So, should I go home and get on my knees to get your attention? We have to talk about what happened." I feel my face get flushed with embarrassment at my own cheekiness.

"No, actually we do not," he replies with an authority that supersedes any emotion or inflection. Deedy has always been able to shut me up, even when I didn't know who or what he actually was. He has this posture, this way of being, that makes me want to instantly become a better person. And I don't want to disappoint him. Again.

He continues, "We have nothing to talk about, because what happened did not happen to you, my darling girl. It happened to her. Well, more specifically, to them. And while I am overwhelmingly interested in hearing how you may feel about that, I can't help but think that besides your burning desire to vent whatever emotion you may be feeling, what you really want..." he leans across the desk and looks into my eyes with a fire behind his eyes, "is to start meddling around someone else's journey. And that, darling girl, is not your job." He points at me with a long elegant finger, and then he wags it back and forth as though he is telling a puppy not to jump on the furniture. "Do I have to explain the importance of what you do one more time?" he asks.

All right, so no matter how much time goes by, this is where Deedy and I always end up. I have been part of the welcoming committee in Heaven for the past half century or so. That means my job is to gather together families and loved ones and be a kind of event planner for new arrivals. Remember when I said that getting to Heaven was a great party? Well, that is partially because of me. I am quite good at my job, if I do say so myself. Not that I do not want to do more, or to be more. Specifically, to have wings and super powers like Gabby. And I have made that very clear to Deedy, both face to face and in our "evening chats," as he likes to put it. So this is the part where Deedy tells me to learn temperance and to not allow my personal ambition to get in my own way. He has a plan for me, just as he does for each of us, blah, blah, blah.

"No!" I say with desperation. "Because I'm not talking in abstracts here. I am not here to discuss your management concepts or the glass ceiling! I am talking about something much more important!" I am on my feet now, my emotions taking over in my voice and my argument. I realize that my hands are on his desk and now I am staring into his eyes. "I cannot…absolutely cannot allow my best friend to go to Hell!"

Linda and I had been like sisters at one time. My first true friend, who stood by me no matter how big of a shitbird I could be—and you have no idea how big that is. I had a knack in my youth of turning bad behavior into fucking performance art if I really put my mind to it. And even when it backfired in Linda's face, like my drunken toast as her maid of honor at her wedding rehearsal dinner, there was always forgiveness in her heart for me.

In the remote viewing room at the company, I have seen so many lives wasted and even more senseless deaths brought on by a hopelessness that can only be felt by beings trapped in their own cruelness. Linda was never cruel, never even unkind. It was painful to watch her grow old and see the bitterness form and then become her armor and shield against a world that she could no longer understand or participate in, and eventually watch it seep into her very heart. Linda's heart was always a wonder to me, so full of love. As I watched her final days tick by like minutes to someone already eternal, and the understanding that in the end she was going to let the bitterness win, first over Hank and then herself. It was a final testament, but it was the wrong testament to her life. Linda was good. Linda was the best. Why should she be punished when so many others who lived terribly—and yes, I am thinking of myself for a brief moment here—get to be here? My breath is now ragged as my thoughts overwhelm me. I sob now as I sit and put my head on Deedy's desk.

He looks at me, and his expression is one of True Love. It brings me a sort of peace, but it also makes me even sadder. How long will it take for Linda to see that expression? Or to feel his comfort?

"I know it is difficult, Louise," he says softly. "To see someone you care about, especially the way you love Linda, make a decision that could cause herself so much pain. But you also know how this works. You know what is ahead for her, and you know that she will eventually find her way home."

"And in the meantime?" I say through a new set of sobs. Damn Deedy, he always knows how to make me cry.

"In the meantime, you are going to have to let her go," he replies gently.

I take a deep breath and realize that an idea is forming as I begin to speak. It just flows so quickly out of my head I wonder for a moment if it is really mine.

24

"Okay," I begin. "Let's talk about my job classification."

"My darling girl!" he says with surprise. "Are you playing the sympathy card? My best friend just committed a heinous act and is on her way to damnation so I should get a promotion?" He sounds incredulous.

"No. Not a promotion. A demotion," I say with excitement. "Send me back," I say that with a little less excitement. To be totally honest, Hell is not a place anyone actually *wants* to go. In fact, I am pretty sure I just heard Gabby gasp out in the lobby. That almost makes me burst out laughing, but I don't. I just look steadily at Deedy, who is returning my gaze with complete amazement.

"You can't be serious," he says.

"Yup. Don't send me back with no memory and having to wear terrible clothes and stuff. Send me back like the people I worked for and with when I was there the first time. Or like Will! Send me back as a guardian! That would be perfect!" I exclaim.

"How would that be perfect? You realize you cannot be Linda's guardian," he says, barely hiding his own shock at my unexpected request. I take a moment to absorb this, and find a teensy bit of pleasure from the fact that the creation can occasionally still surprise the Creator. Free will extends to the afterlife, and I apparently used mine in vast proportions just now. I don't dwell on it for long, though, because I am now on task like a pit bull with a brand new bone.

"Obviously," I say matter-of-factly.

"She won't even be able to see you most likely," he says thoughtfully. I can see he is now considering all the possibilities. Just as a side note, you never want to play chess with God. He can see all the moves—past, present, and future. I'm pretty sure that is what he is doing now. He is playing about one thousand different chess games simultaneously, with me as the self-administered pawn in all of them.

"I spent thirty-two years in Hell, remember? I think I know how the place works," I say with a twinge of reticence in my voice.

Deedy looks at me very closely, in that way that he does. A way that makes me feel like he is seeing through the imaginary body that I, as do all of us, continue to pretend that we have, and is looking at the bare soul I actually am. He studies me for a long moment and then a look of sadness comes over his face. *Uh-oh,* I think to myself. *Did he just see checkmate?* Then I see a quick look of surprise again, followed by sadness once more. Like the ships passing in the night metaphor, his expressions are so fleeting that I wonder if I imagined them. Then for a split second I am afraid that he is about to just announce that he is going to send me back, not as an employee but as a resident where I can wallow for the next ten thousand years in my own ego and insubordination. But finally there is the look of affection and amusement. Where some would take that with relief and comfort, I of course take it as an invitation to go further.

"And you have to admit," I begin. "I would be so much better at the whole guardian thing than *some* people. I mean, I already know the neighborhood, and I am way better at sneaking around than Will on my worst day!" I look at him and nod my head knowingly.

"And she's back!" he says grandly. "My over-confidant Darling Girl." He looks at me and laughs. "Okay. I will have your assignment tomorrow at eight am." Then he pauses and says more seriously, "Are you sure this is what you want?"

"Fuck yeah!" I say.

He raises his eyebrows at me.

"What? Just preparing to return to the old hood. Gotta talk like that natives, ya know." I try to ignore the fact that he is reaching into his desk drawer for the infamous curse jar. That little bit of masterful smartassery will cost me a quarter. I happily make my donation.

"Ofalus yr hyn yr ydych yn dymuno i fy annwyl" Deedy says to me.

"Speaking of old and language. You know, since I have been in Heaven I've met thousands of people from Wales. Even they don't speak Welsh. Why do you?" I say.

"It doesn't look like it sounds, and it doesn't sound like anything else," he says. "I have always had a soft spot for the more puzzling things in life." Then he looks at me and winks mischievously. "People too."

I bow with a flourish of my hand as if I was on a stage. "Thank you. Thank you very much," I say with my own wink. Then I add with all seriousness, "Really, Deedy. Thank you for this."

"Good luck, Louise. I'll see you tomorrow," he says, and I know I am now officially dismissed.

Smiling, I walk back down the hall. Gabby is waiting for me like a panther waiting to pounce.

"Do you have the slightest idea of what you are doing, Louise?" she asks. There is no anger in her voice. I think she is really concerned for me.

"Apparently not," I say. "I never even considered I would once again have to use an alarm clock." I laugh. Everyone in the entire kingdom knows that the one thing I hated more than the coffee or the wardrobe choices in Hell was the fact that I had to be at work at eight in the morning on the dot every fucking morning.

Gabby puts her hand on my shoulder. Her touch gives me a warming sense of goodwill. "You'll be careful down there, right? It has been so long since you've had to have your guard up."

"Gabby, how many of the people who work in Hell had to go there first?" I ask.

"A few," she answers. "But yes, Louise. You are a unique individual," she says with relief.

"And it should be interesting," I continue. "To see the old neighborhood as a tourist instead of a resident. Might even be fun," I say with as much bravado as I can muster. "At the very least, this time I get to come back here every night." I look at Gabby with now sparkling eyes as tears begin to fill them once again. *This time, I know the way home,* I think to myself, knowing there is no such thing if Gabby is around.

"Exactly," Gabby says with a winning grin.

This time I say what I'm thinking out loud, because I still find it a bit creepy when Gabby is speaking while I am just thinking. "And I'm guessing by Deedy's reaction that there isn't a line of folks outside of his office demanding a demotion?"

"To say the least," she answers, laughing out loud. "Like I said, Louise Patterson, you are one of his most unique creations!"

"I will take that as a compliment," I say as I walk to the elevator and prepare to go back down. I step inside when the doors open and hit the button for the first floor. As the doors begin to close, Gabby turns and reaches out so that her arm stops them from closing completely.

"I almost forgot," she says. "Hank just came through intake. You may want to go say hello to him." Then she allows the doors to close and return me to the street.

CHAPTER THREE

As I walk back to the Company, I ponder Hank's arrival. Will he be glad to see me? Will he understand why he is there? Will whoever takes care of his welcoming tell him that Linda is dead too? And why she isn't with him?

Hank and I were never really close in life. We liked each other well enough, but it was a kind of a forced relationship. Love me, love my dog kind of thing. Each of us would consider the other the "dog" in that scenario. I thought that since I was first, I was more important. He believed that because he was her chosen life partner that superseded our friendship. In reality, neither one of us was correct. Linda's heart had plenty of room for both of us, and she was great at making time for me after her wedding. However, it didn't take me long before I began to understand that Hank had a part of her life that I was not invited to ever be privy to experience. The only consolation I had was that I was the one she used to bitch about him to. Hank and I probably knew more about each other than either of us were comfortable with. Linda told him about all my misadventures, and I got to hear about every marital squabble and every gory detail of their private life.

It suddenly occurs to me that seeing me after all this time may just be a sentimental reminder of the early years of his marriage. To the woman who had just poisoned him to death. I start to feel more and more nervous as I approach the WF&PI building. I vacillate between hoping that he knows about Linda already and wishing that his welcomer may have chosen to omit a few details surrounding their demise.

When I arrive at the Company I move swiftly to the main office, where all assignments show up on a board. All I have to do is speak my name and my designated duties will appear for the day. For the rest of today my schedule is suddenly very blank. Due to, I assume, my sudden reclassification from the Big Guy. So, knowing I can relax and not have to worry that I may be leaving someone in the lurch, I am now free to attend Hank's welcoming party as a guest with a clear conscience. I see my father and mother walking down the hall with another familiar looking couple. "Hey, guys! Wait up!" I yell and sprint to catch up with them. My mom looks gorgeous, as usual with surprisingly thick brown hair. She didn't change it mentally when she came here either. She died with that head of hair. Maybe it was a tad more gray, but not overwhelmingly more. What a looker my mom is! My father's good humor is as evident in the afterlife as it was among the living. His smile gets even wider when I approach.

"Louise! What a surprise to see you out here! I thought you would have already been inside. We are running just a tad late," my mom says. She may be a heavenly being, but she's still the master of the backdoor zinger.

"Me too. I had a meeting with Deedy this morning," I say back smugly. Yes, I know it is terrible to use having a somewhat personal relationship with the boss as a leg up in a discussion with your mother, but what can I say? I didn't get here by the scenic route for being a fabulous person all the time.

"That's fine, sweetheart!" my father chimes in with his booming voice. "What was the meeting about? Are they changing your assignment?" He looks concerned. Dad has always been as interested in my afterlife career as me.

30

"We'll talk later," I say breezily and give him a quick kiss on the cheek. "Right now, as Mom just pointed out, we are late for a party!" I now look at the couple in expectation. I assume someone is going to introduce me.

My mom steps forward to the task. "Louise, you remember Mr. and Mrs. Miller? Hank's parents?" I look at them and feel heat in my face. Mr. Miller not only looks shocked to see me on this side of the pearly gates, he looks as if he may have a heart attack and die for the second time. Mrs. Miller tries to force a small smile at me, but her dislike is obvious as well.

"So…" I say, embarrassed. "I guess there is no chance that you have forgotten me."

The only time I ever met the Millers when we were all breathing was at Linda's wedding. The aforementioned rehearsal dinner where I got inebriated and spoken my mind, and the next day where I showed up in a different dress than planned. The dress I was supposed to wear was designed to make me streamlined and color coordinated with the flowers and sophisticated decor. The dress I showed up in was designed to make me look like a deranged circus clown on shore leave. There was a method to my madness, of course...but I'm sure the Millers were never made aware. Thus, my cemented role as the bad influence, riff-raff of a best pal to their new daughter-in-law was following me beyond the grave.

"I'm sure it's all fine, dear. Please do join us. It really is a glorious occasion!" says Mrs. Miller, shaking off any bad feelings. Not that hearing that my best friend's stupid last act that has sent her to the depths of despair and anguish being described as glorious doesn't make the hairs on the back of my neck stand up and twist a bit, but I get what she is saying. Today is glorious for her, and Mr. Miller, and everyone else who loves Hank and is so relieved that he is finally here. That is the best thing about

Heaven. There really is very little consideration about how one dies, how young or old they are, etc. The things that occupy our minds as living creatures, and as survivors to those who have gone before just doesn't even ping on the meter here. Hank is home, and that is cause for celebration. So, with that in mind, I take Mrs. Miller's arm and escort her into her son's welcoming.

"That's right," I say with a big smile. "We are all in this together now!"

Hank is in the center of the room, looking so much older than he did the last time I was face to face with him, but seeming much more alert and spry than he seemed at the end of his days. He is laughing at something a younger looking man just said to him. He turns and says "I don't remember you being such a card, Grandpa!" Then he laughs again. "Of course, I lost you when I was three, right?" That is the other thing about Heaven. You can't tell who is what age or how they may be related. The young ingénue may in fact be the great aunt of the old woman she is sitting next to. I laugh out loud as I think, for probably the millionth time in the last twenty years, *I love being here!* And I feel a small twinge in the center of my belly as I realize I just volunteered to not be here most of the time for the foreseeable future.

When Hank spots his mom and dad his emotions get the better of him. I step back and stand next to my own father. "How long has it been since he has seen them?" I ask Dad.

"For his dad about forty years. His mom went a few years after that, I think," he replies. "Good, long lives, both of them." He looks down at me and there is a touch of sadness behind his smile. I don't know if that is a memory he is reliving about my death, or the fact that he had to wait an additional thirty years before we could have this kind of reunion due to my stint down under, or finally perhaps he is thinking of Linda too. I reach over and squeeze him tight. We are in mid-embrace when, if you will pardon the expression, all hell breaks loose.

"Louise? Louise Patterson? Is that you?" Hank says as he rushes at me like a running back on a football field. I take a step back, not sure what to expect.

"Hello, Hank," I say cautiously. "It's so nice to—" That is all I can blurt out before he reaches me and wraps his meaty arms around me, squeezing my breath completely from my body.

"Louise, I can't believe I'm looking at you again. It's so great to see you here." He lifts me up like a ragdoll and starts spinning me around, laughing like we are teenagers.

"Hank, my stomach may be imaginary, but I swear I am going to puke if you don't cut it out!" I scream through my own laughter.

"Sorry, Lou," Hank replies, breathless now as he puts me down. "I just keep forgetting that we are still old folks. I feel so young." Then he stops and really looks at me. "But look at you. You are still young. And pretty as a picture!" he says with true admiration.

I don't know whether to be uncomfortable or flattered. "I don't remember you being such a charmer, back when I was alive." My surprise came through my newly high pitched voice.

"Well," he started, teasing me. "Way back then you scared the shit out of me!" A look of slight panic entered his eyes, and I start to laugh out loud.

"Don't worry, cussing doesn't disqualify you. But it will cost you a quarter. Really. I wish I was kidding, but I can show you my personal bank statements that will prove to you exactly how much it can add up to," I say.

Now it is his turn to laugh. "Why doesn't that shock me? Oh yeah, because I know you."

"So, why did I seem scary to you?" I question.

"Let's see, you were Linda's trash-talking, anti-establishment, marriage-hating best friend."

Once again, my face starts to flush with embarrassment. "I guess I have owed you an apology for a very long time."

"Not at all. You are partially responsible for creating the person I spent most of my life with. For that, you don't owe me anything at all," he answered, his blush rising to meet mine.

Fuck me running. So he doesn't know, or doesn't remember. Will someone else tell him while he is at his welcoming party? Should I hope someone does, or would it be better coming from me? These questions are running through my head as Hank leans close to my ear.

"But, Lou, I have some questions that I am not really comfortable asking anyone else." He looks around quickly, like he is about to say something terribly secret or perhaps off-color. "I know these people are family, but they all feel strange to me." He looks at me hopefully.

"I'll be happy to help in any way," I say. "I'm taking a new assignment tomorrow, so I won't be available during the day. If you don't mind waiting until the evening, we can make plans to get together?"

"That is awesome of you, Lou," he says with gratitude. "I would not only be willing to wait, I will look forward to it." Hank sounds so pleased, like he was my best friend, not married and eventually killed by her.

"Me too," I say warmly. "But for now, enjoy your party and spend some time with people you haven't seen in a while." I stand and open my arms to embrace him. "You are going to be very happy here," I whisper in his ear.

"Tomorrow night," he says through eyes that are starting to fill. "Don't forget!"

"No worries. I will be here," I say, then suddenly

remembering where I will be coming from, I add, "And I could quite possibly have bells on!" He does not get my half-joke, but I make a promise to myself that I'll explain tomorrow night.

I start to move through the room, waving cordially to folks I do not know and stopping to say hi to those that I do. I stop and give my mom a hug and a kiss. I am not surprised when my dad insists on walking me out. We make our escape quietly and walk arm-in-arm toward my condo. It is just a few blocks and the weather, as usual, is perfect. We walk by my old place of employment IP&FW—Internet Porn and Fetish Web—the only internet service available in Hell. I worked in their call center when I first arrived.

You see, Heaven and Hell exist within the same space. We actually sometimes walk the same streets, live in adjoining neighborhoods, everything. The difference is the residents. While the majority of Hellions live on the opposite side of the city, and a great deal of Heaven's occupants live…well…up, we basically are all the same. With the help of Deedy's magic, residents of Hell can't see anything that would be considered Heaven-centric. The heat that makes Hell such a famous shit hole is manufactured by the guilt and remorse that people who feel they belong there walk around carrying with them. Isn't that a kick in the teeth? Most people go to Hell because they feel that they deserve it.

And the ones that were so bad in life that there was no choice but eternal damnation? They have a very special punishment. With all its torments, Hell would be a playground to mass murderers, pedophiles, dictators, and tyrants. They come here not only under tortuous circumstances, but also as children. The most frightening thing about Hell is the kid population. I happen to have first-hand knowledge of that particular fact. One of my temp jobs was at a daycare center in Hell.

However, it was my work at IP&FW that truly gave me insight into the general population. Hell is the one place in the entire universe that everyone without exception needs a Xanax, and it's the one place where you cannot find one. No peace, no rest, no "tomorrow is a better day." Not until you have learned whatever lessons your soul desires and Deedy finds you and brings you home. And since no one there knows or expects that to happen, the despair can be suffocating.

My dad was the only member of my immediate family that was there to greet me when I got to Heaven. I didn't have a welcoming party, because I didn't come straight there. But having him standing with open arms was so special. Some people thought I was a daddy's girl in life, but that doesn't hold a candle to what I am in the afterlife.

I remember in second grade, this classmate of mine, a precocious little girl called Kimmy with huge brown eyes that apparently made every adult in the room turn into a mass of goo. Kimmy was sitting next to me at lunch, for some strange reason. We weren't exactly friends, but I guess at that age, we weren't self-aware enough to consider each other enemies. Anyway, I looked up from my peanut butter and jelly to realize that my father was walking across the cafeteria with my homework in his hand. I had forgotten it that morning on the counter, and I was already prepared for the wrath of Mrs. Newman, but now my dad was coming to save me. I remember how shocked I felt when I saw him standing among my classmates and teachers. I guess when you are eight years old, compartmentalization of your life comes naturally. It was very strange for me to see someone from my home, my oasis from the chaos, standing among the rest of the captives in my daytime cage. Yes, I felt that strongly about the educational institution even at that tender age. After Daddy had handed me the precious papers that were basically a get out of jail free card to me, he leaned over and gave me a quick kiss, then turned and left. Without the papers in my hand I could have believed that I had imagined the entire experience. That is, until Kimmy turned to me with those big brown eyes and said, "Your dad is kinda funny looking, isn't he?" An innocent comment from a child's perspective would be the first thought of any reasonable adult. My father himself, if he had heard it would have laughed out loud. However, for a rival child, those words were a declaration of war. The look of shock and horror were the last expression those adorable eyes were able to make for the remainder of the week. Particularly the left one, which was swollen shut after I pounded it with my tiny fists of fury. I felt like Chuck Norris. Chuck Norris sitting in the principal's office, but it was pretty intoxicating nevertheless. Now, take that level of devotion and times it by ten and that is where I am today.

Dad and I are laughing at that shared memory as we enter my apartment building.

The access point for each condo is located in a common hallway shared by all condos in that building. Much like Hell, I'm not bothered by my neighbors, but unlike Hell we all get along. I have always believed my sanctuary to be unique, even though there are at least twelve units in this building. Upon entering my tiny yet elegant space, I am immediately put at rest with its interior painted in the softest of pale blues and the deep plush wall to wall carpet. We enter into the living room where I am greeted by the only wall within its protective boundaries. It is L-shaped, made of mortar and stone providing a warmth like no simple wall I have ever seen. Within its confines there is a glass fireplace that allows viewing from the oversized sofa strategically placed in front of it or the overstuffed grandmother's bed that I slumber so peacefully in directly on the other side where my bedroom is located. And this bedroom has ample walk-in closet space graciously giving me several choices of fabulous outfits each day. The dining area houses simply a large tabled booth, which gives it a sense of style as well as some retro funkiness that always makes me feel super cool. Lastly, the tiny white kitchen with its pristine tiled countertops and small appliances is housed by a far wall made completely of glass. Standing in the kitchen I look out to the most breathtaking view. We aren't up terribly high, but we are high enough that Hellions would be blinded before they ever caught a glimpse of me through the wall. But when I look through it, it looks as if my apartment sits on the top of a rainbow. This rainbow was not preceded by a storm, it never disappears, its colors never fade. It stands eternal, just like Deedy's promise that there is room for everyone here, and everyone is coming home someday. I offer my father a glass of water; pure, delicious, and ice cold straight from the tap. He accepts and sits on the couch.

"Can I get you something else? Something to eat?" I ask casually.

"How about information. What is up, Lou?" His face is suddenly filled with that fatherly concern again.

I laugh out loud. "What are you worried about, Dad?"

"What I have always worried about when it comes to you." He downs his glass of water in one long, breathless draw. "That your mouth is writing checks that your ass can't cash. And the fact that I noticed Linda was not with Hank when he arrived today, I am thinking that check was drawn from the National Bank of Hell."

"Okay, yes...my new assignment is back there," I start slowly. "But it isn't like I'm being sent back to eternal damnation. This time I will be there as an employee."

Dad stares at the bottom of his empty glass. "Still, it feels a little like a demotion, doesn't it, Louise?"

"But can you really call it a demotion if I asked for the assignment?" I answer him quietly.

"I knew it!" he exclaims. "You think you are going to save Linda!" He leaps off the sofa and for a split second I honestly believe he is about to spank me like I am six years old again with my hand stuck in the forbidden cookie jar.

Fortunately he stops short and instead puts his hand on the side of my face, cupping my cheek. "Are you crazy, baby girl?" he says.

"Maybe, but I'm delusional. I know I can't save her. I just feel better knowing that even though she's there and I am here we can share the same space sometimes. The chance of me even seeing her is one in a million, and the chance of her seeing me is non-existent. It really is more about me than it is her. Understand?"

"Nope. But what else is new." He sighs heavily. "Just promise me you will let me know if you get in over your head? If you begin to feel overwhelmed?" His concern is palatable. My eyes start to feel wet and my vision blurs. I blink quickly to stave off the tears. My love for this man is the only thing overwhelming me right now.

"I love you, Daddy, but sometimes I really feel like I need to introduce myself." I laugh and give him a peck on the cheek. "I'm lazy, I have been known to be a mooch, particularly off of you and Mom back in the day, and I have been called a slacker more than once. But have you ever known me to get in over my head? Well, at least for me to admit it?"

Now he is laughing. "No. You have always been the bravest person I know."

"Then give me a little credit. It is all going to be fine." We embrace, and I rest my head on his chest. I imagine feeling his heartbeat, even though I know that there isn't one. I take a deep breath and give him another squeeze. "Now I have to kick you out. Early day tomorrow!" I say cheerily.

"Good night, sweetie. And good luck tomorrow." He walks out the door, and I close it behind him. There is no need to lock it. We don't even have locks on our doors up here. No peep holes either. What threatening thing could be waiting outside a door in paradise?

I move to the bedroom and feel the temperature drop. Even though the space is open, the temperature in the bedroom is always freezing cold. I love to sleep in a cold room. Everything here is exactly how you want it to be. I get into my pajamas, which are also my ideal. Large and fleecy and soft. Then, almost out of habit I get on my knees by the bed and fold my hands in front of me.

I sit there and think for just a moment. Then I finally say, "Hello, Deedy. Not much too really say tonight. Guess I will see you bright and early in the morning." Then I laugh and crawl into bed.

It's funny, but in Heaven I rarely dream. If I were ever to have a gun pointed at my head, with some crazy person demanding that I must come up with one thing I miss about Hell, this would be the only thing I could say. In Hell, dreams were all I had. In Heaven we have everything we could possibly dream of, hence…no actual real dreams.

Except for tonight.

Tonight my peaceful slumber turns into a confessional of my true motivation for asking Deedy for the new job. I would be embarrassed if I were awake, but my subconscious apparently has no shame. In my dream I appear in Hell as a fearless and respected warrior. I fly through the streets on mighty wings. People scatter when they see me approaching. Sinners fall to the ground and weep when they see me, calling my name and turn to each other saying things like "She used to be one of us, but look at her now!" But I don't have time to stop and bask in their adoration. I'm searching every face, looking for Linda. I call out to her as I swoop down corner to corner, through alleys and shops. Finally, I see her walking toward me. She's young again, nineteen or twenty. She looks like she looked when we first met at a party so many years ago. At first she seems confused, looking at the people surrounding her with bewilderment. Then her eyes scan me, and recognition lights up her face. "Lou?" she cries. "Lou, I don't know what happened. Please tell me you are here to save me!" she pleads.

"Of course I am," I say in this weird, amplified voice. I land next to her and take her hand. "Did you really think I would let you stay here?" She smiles and gazes at me with pure admiration and gratitude.

"Come on," I say as we rise together, my gorgeous wings strong enough to support us both. "Let's go be happier today than we were yesterday, and make all our tomorrows wonderful." And holding on to my best friend, I fly into the bright blue sky.

CHAPTER FOUR

Linda wakes to find herself in a strange hotel-like room. There is even a neon sign outside flashing the words NO VACANCY right outside her window, making the dark space seem like a slow motion video of a disco from the 1970s. She shakes the cobwebs out of her head and sits up. There is no TV, and she is not in her recliner. Then she remembers. She is not at home, and she will never be there again. "I'm dead," she says aloud to the silent flashing. "And so is Hank." She looks around, almost panicky, but registers a bit of disappointment too when she realizes she's alone.

Everything in this room is gray. A washed out, colorless, threadbare bedspread thrown over an ancient mattress. Linda gets up and looks at it with disgust. *This makes "Don't let the bed bugs bite" sound like an actual threat.* There is a small table in the corner with a dusty old monitor sitting on top. "Internet? Seriously?" There is also a chair, but it looks like it would collapse under the weight of a newspaper, let alone her. There is a closet and there seems to be something hanging in it. Linda looks down and realizes she is currently naked. Not that it is uncomfortable, since she has A) come to terms with her aged body and B) realizes that it has to be one hundred and twelve degrees at least in this miserable room, but she still pulls open the door and sees a dress made out of the same material as the bedspread. It is fantastically horrid. She looks at the size and it is at least four sizes too big. She stops to wonder what happen to Tara O'Fatass that she left behind her dress that she made from an extra blanket, one could only assume. Maybe her Clark Gable came and carried her away. Linda looks around one more time. "Yeah, probably not."

She decides to stay naked for now and moves to the bathroom. The stench is so bad it is like an actual thing inside the room. She can feel it. She gags and flushes the toilet, which also had remnants of a former guest left behind inside of it. She searches for air freshener or at least soap to cut into the lingering stench. There is absolutely nothing in here. No little shampoos, no fancy soap, not even a free shower cap or one of those shitty little sewing kits with four pieces of thread and a single button too small to fit anything inside. "This place makes a roach motel look like a fucking Hilton!" she exclaims. "And why is it so hot?" With that she gets a flash of realization. She slides onto the floor and starts to cry. "Fuck me. I am in Hell," she cries.

After about fifteen minutes of steady sobbing, she pulls herself together and gets up, walks over and rips a thin strip off of the remaining bedspread, and uses it to tie up her hair. Then she walks over to the closet, gets out the dress and pulls it over her head. There are combat boots at the bottom of the closet that she pulls onto her feet. For a brief moment she wonders where Hank is right now, and wishes he was here to provide her with some comfort in his familiarity if nothing else. But no, she is glad he isn't here and hopes in her heart of hearts that he ended up somewhere better. She wipes the remaining tears from her face and walks to the door.

She flashes on some old movie she watched one night when she couldn't sleep and is afraid that she may not be able to leave this room. But when she pulls open the door and enters the hallway, nothing pulls her back in. So, she continues down two flights of stairs and into the lobby.

Even through the dingy windows of the lobby she can tell that the air outside is kind of orangey. She wonders if that's fire on the other side of the door. She stops at the front desk where a man of about forty is on the computer behind the counter. He is beating the side of it and cursing under his breath. She stands and waits patiently for a few minutes, then with no sign of his personal battle ending any time soon, she clears her throat.

He looks at her with disgust. "What?"

She realizes she has no idea what she's about to say. She just opens her mouth and waits to see what comes out. "I don't know what to do now," she whispers.

"You are the newbie in room twenty-four, right?" he responds, with no less disdain.

"Guess so," she answers.

"Well, I suggest you get your ass out there and find a job. Because rent is due by the end of the week."

"A job?" She is in wonder now. She has not had a job in years. She's in her 80s for fuck's sake.

"Yeah, like what I'm doing right now? You think I hang out behind the counter of a Hellion half-way house for fun?" She is really not liking this kid at all.

"Where should I go?" she asks, not really expecting any help at all.

"Anywhere but here, grandma," he says with his eyes on the computer again.

With that, her last shred of doubt diminishes, and she knows this is it. It's time to face her eternity. So she turns and walks out the door into the streets of Hell.

CHAPTER FIVE

My first thought is why does eight am come so damn early in the morning? Granted, I am not fully conscious at this point. But then I become fully aware and much to my own surprise, a little excited. Yes, I am headed to a scary new assignment. But it is also a new adventure. And of course, after last night's dream, I can secretly admit that I am hoping to run into Linda once I get there.

There's the rub. I can secretly wish whatever I want, but I can never speak that wish aloud. Of course Deedy and Gabby will know. Hell, they may have already known before I ever did. But until it is spoken and made real, it belongs to me and me alone. That is how things work both here and in the living world. Each of us is gifted with a sacred chamber deep within our spirit where we can run free. Free of judgment, free of criticism. No wish or thought can be held against a person while it is kept there.

Once you say it, or worse, act on it, do something to turn it into a thing instead of a concept, then and only then is Karmic Debt incurred. In other words, you can wish your lying, cheating, bitch of an ex-wife die a slow and painful death, but you ain't allowed to kill her.

I hop out of bed and move to the bathroom where I take a moment to run a very hot shower. I like the way the steam rises and clings to the glass and chrome fixtures, coating everything with clean. I always enjoy this, but today in particular it is nice. Because today I won't see fresh or clean for many hours.

I stand in the shower and let the hot water run over my body, my face, my hair. I enjoy the last real comfort of the day before I step out and wrap myself in a large, incredibly fuzzy towel. I make my way to my closet. In the last few years, me and my closet have developed a love affair. Every day I not only get choices, but they are amazing choices. Designer couture, long breezy maxi-dresses, full legged pantsuits in soft linen, intricately embroidered jackets. Yes, I have my own signature style in Heaven. And the shoes! The shoes alone are worth the price of admission. Peep toe stilettos, adorable kitten heels, soft buttery leather flats, like little pieces of art you can wear on your feet.

However, today our love affair turns into an 'I think we should see other people' kind of relationship. To be specific, I think my closet is fooling around with whatever supernatural power runs the closets in Hell. I look in dismay at my only choice for the day. To be fair, it is not as bad as the Hellions are finding in their closets right now, but it will definitely blend in with their daily punishment.

It seems to be a sort of uniform. Navy blue pants that are stiff with starch and have been creased to the point of looking like they have seams sewn down them. There is a light blue cotton shirt that looks worn at the collar and the bottom of the sleeves. While it is faded, it is also soft and looks reasonably comfortable. Thankfully, there is not a name patch above the front pocket. I put on the plain white underwear supplied for me and then the uniform. I tuck in the shirt and find a belt in the back that works well to separate the two blues if not to hold up the pants, that seem to fit me perfectly. I also find a pair of white tube socks that I put on, laughing because Bobby, the love of my life, would refuse to wear anything but these ridiculous socks. I didn't even have to match them up after doing laundry. I would just open up a drawer and dump an entire basket of the same sock into the drawer. He claimed it was easier to get dressed every morning. I thought it was a fashion impediment. Today, however, I look at those socks and want to kiss them. Finally, there is a pair of boots at the bottom of the closet that are heavy and steel toed, but surprisingly supportive and even kind of bouncy under my feet. Okay, so it's no white Chanel suit with a high neck and a pencil skirt, but it is still from Heaven after all. I run a brush through my hair, pinch my cheeks, glance at my reflection in the mirror—yes, mirrors work even though our bodies are kind of imaginary. I think the mirrors might be too, but that is just my theory—blow myself a kiss and walk out the door.

When I arrive at the Second Chance Temp Agency Gabby is waiting, coffee in hand, with a huge smile plastered across her face. It looks unnatural, like she is secretly Mrs. Potato Head and she has just picked up that smile and crammed it into her face seconds before I got there.

"Should I be frightened?" I ask.

"Why?" she answers sweetly. "I just figured you wouldn't have time to chat while coffee brewed, since you didn't arrive until two minutes to eight for an eight o'clock appointment."

Good grief. I had forgotten about Gabby's almost compulsive need for punctuality. "So that's it? You are worried about my being on time?"

"Of course it is!" she says, and that smile gets even wider, against all biological possibility. Gabby is not being 100 percent honest.

Suddenly it strikes me. She saw my dream. My arrogant, ambitious dream that pretty much proves I was lying my ass off when I swore that was not why I wanted to go back to Hell.

"Gabby, I can explain my—"

"Inability to get up and moving on time?" she interrupts me gently. "Too bad, you'll have to save your excuses for your next visit. You are officially out of time.

The boss will be bellowing down the hall any second now." Her smile is now kind, but her eyes are screaming at me. And I don't need telepathic powers to get the message loud and clear. Shut up, Louise. Shut up now. Keep your secrets safe.

"I understand," I say with gratitude. "Thanks for the coffee." The delicious brew is halfway to my mouth when Deedy's voice intrudes into our unspoken conversation.

"Where is that darling girl? I tell you something, Gabby, you are slipping. You used to be so much more on point, keeping my appointments running on time!" I can hear laughter in his voice. I think it is funny that Deedy has noticed her whole prompt issue too.

"Don't let him get away with that, Gabrielle!" I say loudly, but also with humor. Then I storm through the door into his office and announce, "Honey, I'm home!"

Deedy laughs out loud. "My goodness, Ms. Patterson, you are in an awfully good mood, considering what is about to happen."

"And what is about to happen?" I say eagerly, pulling up a chair across from his desk.

Deedy strides over to his desk and lets his long body fold into the chair. Then he reaches into a drawer and pulls out a file. I used to hate that when I worked here. Those file folders house every bit of information regarding a person's life, death, afterlife, even dreams. When I was still under the false impression that Deedy was a weird temp agency owner, I was still very aware that he had some kind of access. He knew all of my baggage, some of it that was lost to me, in my remorse ridden brain. He now looks over the file in front of him, and I realize he is peering into the very soul of some poor schmuck who is as clueless as I used to be.

Deedy looks up and smiles at me. "You are assigned to be the guardian..." He pauses after saying the word guardian and gives me a half beat to rise up and say that I've changed my mind. I look at him defiantly to let him know that is not going to happen.

"...of a man named Joe Watkins," he continues. "Joe died tragically. He was very young. Thirty-five."

"Wow, so this could be a cool assignment after all. Got a picture of the kid?" I say flirtatiously.

"He is older than you, Louise. And he has been in Hell for over seventy years. Believe me, he is not in the mood for a blind date with an ambitious little sprite who thinks she can talk her way through a keyhole." He winks at me.

"You don't mean that. You love me," I say teasingly.

"I mean every word, and of course I love you," he answers.

"So, thirty-five. What happened to Joe?"

"Car accident. Unfortunately, it was on a very bad day."

"What happened?"

"Joe was a journalist, back in the day when print was king, no one had heard of the internet yet, and tabloid journalism was enjoying a certain amount of dubious prestige. Like a bastard son of an emperor suddenly coming into his birthright," Deedy says.

"So he worked for the National Enquirer?" I ask and then tap on the lid of the curse jar expectantly, imitating the way Deedy always does it when I use a curse word.

"Actually, he worked for a small budget wanna-be tell all paper. And, Ms. Sassy Pants, I used the term bastard in its original, Germanic context. Not as a curse." Deedy loves words, all words, even some of the worst ones. And he always knows where they came from and what they are supposed to mean. "Anyway," he continues, "do you remember an actor named Tom Thomas?"

"Of course, everyone knew Tom Thomas," I exclaim.

"He was like, every girl's dream man when my mom and her friends were teenagers." I stop to reflect on when he died. "I was in my late teens when he passed. For a minute I actually thought he may have been a long lost relative, the way my mom reacted. And the phone was ringing off the hook with all her cronies calling to cry and sob and beat their chests over his death. Then I thought that maybe my mom had actually dated him, because my dad got all irritated at Mom and her friends, and walked around the house muttering stuff like 'What kind of man has the same name two times, anyway.' And 'I hated him in that movie with the dog. The dog had more talent.' Once I found out that he was just my mom's favorite actor, I sort of thought she was being silly, but I also remember thinking that that was the closest I ever got to seeing my mother as a real person, not just a mom." I smile now at that memory.

"Do you remember how he died?" Deedy asks.

"Drug overdose. Big surprise," I say with sarcasm.

Deedy looks at me questioningly. So I continue, "He was a celebrity. All celebrities die of a drug overdose, murder, drowning in their own pool, or psoriasis of the liver," I say matter-of-factly, as though everyone in the universe has come to the same conclusion.

"Wow, that's a broad generalization," Deedy says, casually.

"So what does Tom Thomas have to do with our Joe?" I ask.

"Joe was the reporter who scooped the biggest exclusive of that year. Maybe even of that century."

I reach into the deepest caverns of my memory, searching for the old dusty jar marked "Useless pop culture facts from when I was alive."

"Yeah," I say. "That Tom Thomas, my mom's generation's biggest heartthrob since Elvis Presley, was as gay as a picnic basket?" The memory came back suddenly.

"And unlike most of Joe's stories, he did not have to rely on his own imagination credited as a source close to the star. He had a spurned lover with photographic evidence to out Mr. Thomas. It was a glorious victory for him and his paper." Deedy has just a touch of edge in his voice.

"So he didn't lie, and he did his job. He did it well, so it would seem. How does that constitute a bad day?" I realize I am literally sitting on the edge of my seat. I scoot back and wait for an answer.

"Because it was the day after that exclusive hit the streets that Tom went to visit his neighbor. The neighbor was a somewhat famous drummer for an up and coming rock band. He was able to supply enough heroin for Tom to end his life." Deedy looks up and finishes the story looking directly at me. "That was the first and only time Tom had ever done heroin. While all the papers, legitimate and tabloid, reported it as another celebrity doing too much of his favorite drug, most everyone in the inner circle suspected suicide."

"But why?" I ask incredulously. "Why did he feel that was the only way out? By the time the story came to light his career was long over, and the stigma regarding a gay actor playing straight roles was a faded memory."

"My darling girl, you too died young, so you never knew the sensation of growing old. The world changes around you, adopts new ideas and accepts new things, but people rarely do. Even though the world could take Tom Thomas being gay, Tom couldn't live in a world where he was out. All he knew was his secrets, the compartmentalization of his private and public lives."

"So back to Joe," I respond quietly.

"Joe had cultivated some real relationships during his

career. That is what he was known for, having actual sources. It didn't take long before he realized the whispers about Tom and suicide were true."

"And he felt like he had single handedly ruined a man's life," I finish with conviction.

"He felt like he had single handedly ended a man's life," Deedy says. "He went to a local bar, planning to drink until he felt better, or until he forgot altogether. When the bar closed and he hadn't accomplished either of those goals, he got into his car and drove home."

"That didn't work out either," I say.

Deedy closes the file folder and slips it back into the desk. He folds his hands under his chin, a move I've seen so many times. "The thing is, Lou, if he had never written that story, never had to endure the horrific consequences, his life would have gone so differently. There was a path he could have taken that would have given him prestige and fame. There was another one where he might have become a novelist and won awards. There was one where he got married and lived in a small town running a local paper that wrote about little league tournaments and pot luck dinners."

I can see the pain in his eyes. I have never heard him talk this way. I never realized that the chess game he plays in his head is seeing not just what was, what is, and what will be. He can see everything that could have been. I can't imagine how his heart breaks every moment of every day as he watches us, his creations, make choices that lead us away from him and into despair.

"I understand why he ended up in Hell, but why was he there so long before he got this shot?" I wonder aloud.

"Because at his core, Joe is a good man. When he passed he was filled with so much shame and grief that he could not see any good at all within himself. That brand of ruefulness takes a long time to work through."

I get a fleeting thought that I must express. "Are you saying that because I was an awful person, but didn't feel as guilty as Joe, I was able to escape fire and brimstone in half the time?" My tone sounds a bit more accusing that I intend.

"No," Deedy says in a tired voice. "In fact I was not, if you can possibly believe such a thing, referring to you in any way. I was talking about Mr. Watkins, the guy who is still as of this hour, in the land of eternal suffering."

"Okay, fine. But can I ask a question that is sort of about me?" I ask.

"Of course," Deedy says, laughing now.

"Besides follow him around, what exactly are my duties?"

That question did the trick. Deedy is now back to his usual effervescence. "Believe it or not, I need you to be as bad as Will when it comes to following him around. It's a very fine line. Don't look completely incompetent but just make sure he knows he is being watched."

"Okay, why?"

"Tell me you didn't feel just a little better when you knew Will was around? When you felt there was always a pair of eyes on you?"

"Yeah, that was nice," I admit.

"And when the time comes, I'll need you to stay close and protect him. You know how it is at the end. Things might get a little hairy." Deedy is suddenly serious.

"Is he going to have to go to the Day Care Center?" Even I can hear the fear in my voice. Those memories are still a little too fresh for me.

"His experience will be different, but you will still know," he answers.

"Right," I say breezily, standing. "Easy Peasy Mac and Cheesy! Where do I start?"

Deedy gives me one of his signature smiles. "And you accuse me of talking rubbish. Downstairs with you, Ms. Elevator Repair Person. He should be arriving for the first time in about a half an hour." Deedy stands and approaches me. "And now, my darling girl, this is goodbye until the end of the assignment."

"Why?" I ask with panic. "I thought I was able to return to Heaven every night!"

"Relax, you will. But you won't be able to see or talk to me. And I'm sorry, Lou, but I have to do this." He puts his hand over my eyes and through the blackness I hear him say "hwyl fawr."

"I know that one! That means goodbye," I say as the sensation of his hands on my face disappears. When I open my eyes the room is empty. Not just without Deedy, but nothing is there. No desk, no chairs, no files. "Deedy?" I call into the nothingness around me. There is no answer. I feel a chill run down my spine.

I spin and rush out of the office, hurling myself down the hall toward Gabby. When I see her I feel a surge of relief. "Gabby!" I exclaim and realize after I speak that I am screaming.

Gabby turns and floats toward me.

Floats.

Like when I first met her. She no longer has wings.

I remember the first time I saw her in Heaven, my surprise at her seemingly new accoutrement. "Gabby!" I had said. "You grew wings!"

"I've always had wings, Louise. You just couldn't see them before now." She had explained to me, all those years ago.

Now she looks like she did then. I start to hyperventilate. Gabby rushes over to me and puts her hands on my shoulders. "Don't panic, Lou. It is just protocol."

"Am I back to being totally blind?" I say, rushing over to the windows to peer out.

When I was in Hell, looking up was like looking directly into the sun. Today my eyes are painfully reminded of those days. There is no more beauty in my world, just blinding light and nothing else.

"Gabby, I don't like this!" I turn, now sightless for a minute while my eyes adjust.

"It's okay, Louise. It is just camouflage. Joe has to be able to see and interact with you, and you have to fit in as much as possible. Try not to worry."

Try not to worry? Riddle me this, angel girl.

"Can Heaven really be Heaven if you can't see God?"

CHAPTER SIX

Joe pulls on his clothes by rote, barely paying attention to the almost comedic ridiculousness of the outfit. After all these years, nothing can surprise him anymore. If he is being honest with himself, he really doesn't care either.

He hasn't really cared about a whole lot for the last, who knows how long. A dozen years? A hundred years? Fifteen minutes? Time means nothing in eternity. And down here, what would be the point in trying to track it anyway? There are no holidays, technically you no longer have a birthday after you are dead, and the only thing that separates day from night is the tossing and turning of a few sleepless hours compared to abject misery and a thankless job in the wakeful ones.

Thinking about work makes Joe's head hurt. His brain is still reeling over recent events. He cannot believe that after all this time, however much time that may be, he summarily lost the only job he's known not only in death but in life. Joe stops to remember when he first bit the proverbial dust. Once he realized that hell was an awful lot like any earthly city, only with shittier people and a much higher heat index, he found his way to the offices of the one thing that every earthly city, no matter how big or how small, has to have. A newspaper. Once he had walked into the editor's office and announced what he had done to find himself sentenced to eternal fire and brimstone, he was hired on the spot. Since then, Joe has found himself spending every day of his afterlife on the city desk of the Hellion Gazette. His job was mainly writing stories cunningly designed to make everyone, well at least everyone who would buy and read a paper down here, feel even more miserable than they had before they read it. The circulation stayed relatively low, compared to the population. Readers were mostly newbies who buy the paper out of habit, since that was what they did when they were alive. Even after the boxes with the disgusting websites showed up, the numbers remained steady. Of course, it always spiked a little every once in a while, and Joe had learned that was probably the month of January back in the land of the living. Just one of the many fascinating facts Joe had learned while working at the Gazette. More people die in January than any other month. People also die more often at the beginning of every month than the end. And if you are looking to be a true part of the "in crowd," you'll want to die at eleven in the morning.

Anyway, Joe was a natural from jump. He had even gotten some hate mail for his work, which in Hell is the equivalent to a Pulitzer Prize. Yesterday started like any other day, sitting in the editor's office getting the day's miserable assignments. The editor with the gruff voice of a lifelong smoker, asking who wants to write a story about the thirty-fifth anniversary of the construction on 7th avenue. Joe passed on that one. He had written the story about the thirtieth anniversary of the construction on 7th avenue. Was that really five years ago? Seems like yesterday. He offered the story to the guy who got the assignment. All he had to do was go through it and change all the thirtys to thirty-fives. Put in a few fives and go home early. The next story on the block was an expose of one of the superstores at the edge of town. Specifically, how long it takes to get out of the store once you walk through the doors and make the dreadful choice to actually make a purchase. Some folks have claimed standing in line for as long as six days. Joe leaped at the opportunity to finally get the chance to write about the superstore. With its piss poor customer service, the shoddy products, and the exorbitant amount of makeup the women who work there seem to be forced to wear. All of this under the roof of a great white elephant is exactly what poses as a shopping experience in Hell. He was thrilled when the editor handed him the blue post-it note with the assignment written on it. This was going to be his most depressing story to date. And it will practically write itself.

Joe virtually skipped to the superstore. He was that excited. His adrenaline was pumping like it used to when he worked as a member of the paparazzi. The word paparazzi is Italian meaning "large mosquito." While most would say that is because they represent annoying blood sucking versions of journalistic bottom feeders, he would argue that it is because of the buzz he heard in his ears whenever he was chasing a good story. That buzzing was happening now and Joe knew he was going to nail it.

That is, until he arrived. Once he got through the doors he saw something, something he was not expecting to ever see here. Sure there was plenty of fodder for a real "down in the mouth" story that would drive every reader into an abyss of hopelessness. The fact that it took several tries to get through the electronic door, the guy standing in the middle of aisle nine screaming to the top of his lungs, the unsupervised toddler dumping containers of various liquids while frightened workers stood around too terrified of the diminutive demon to approach him. Joe took out his reporter's notebook, prepared to start scribbling about how wretched every aspect of this place was. Instead, he turned his attention to a small group that seemed to be actually enjoying themselves. Unlike the rest of Hell, where folks either avoided one another or were downright vicious to their fellow residents, these people were smiling, and laughing, and talking. Joe realized it had been so very long since he had heard laughter, seen another human being smile. He was drawn to these people like a starving man to a smorgasbord. He was starved, but not from lack of food. He was starved of human emotion. He sat with them and started to listen. These folks had taken an opportunity, while waiting in this endless line, to build relationships. For some unknown reason, these people had decided to suspend the general misery that the overbearing heat and despair that followed them everywhere, even into this store. Perhaps the additional frustrations had been just enough to cause an opposing effect, like temporal aliasing makes wheels in movies and on television seem to be going backward. Joe found himself writing down things like 'Long lines help alleviate the loneliness of Hell' and 'Every living soul, even those of us with sentences to eternal damnation, apparently retains a capacity for Joy.'

If someone were to ask him why, even today, he would not be able to answer. He played the events of yesterday over and over in his head, and other than temporary insanity, he truly is without defense. He has no idea why those people seemed happy, and he is clueless as to why he was so compelled to document that happiness as completely as he had. All he knows is that when he got back to the office and spent a few hours typing it up and handing in the story, the editor perused it, looked at him as though he was looking at a stranger, and handed him his pink slip.

Terminated for inciting peace and good will.

Once Joe had gotten over the shock of being fired, and wrapped his head around the fact that he had lost the one job he thought was his calling, he began to clean out his desk. It was there, among a pile of papers and old notebooks that a strange post-it note appeared. Unlike his usual blue ones from the editor, this one was yellow. On it was printed in perfect penmanship:

DO YOU BELONG HERE?
CALL US TO FIND OUT!
SECOND CHANCE TEMP AGENCY
(666)-573-2236

He considered this and shoved the post-it into the box with the rest of his "personal belongings." Then he had gotten up and faced the open stares of his co-workers, giving them all a middle finger of their very own. Then he wondered if one of them had placed the post it on his desk as a gesture of kindness. After looking back at each of their faces, he decided that was probably not the case. This felt like a secret. It felt…special. None of these bozos would qualify as kind or special. As he was walking out the door for the last time, he had to squelch the overwhelming desire to stop by the editor's office and take a giant shit right on his desk. Laughing at the thought of the expressions on everyone's face if he gave into that prepossession, he heard someone call his name. He turned and saw an old buzzard of a man who had only been working there for a few weeks. Joe seemed to think his name was Doug, but he could not guarantee it, so he just answered, "What?"

"Phone for you, Watkins," he barked. "I told her you'd been canned, but she says it is urgent and it has to be you."

Joe goes back to his now empty desk and picks up the phone. "Joe Watkins, City Desk," he said, out of pure habit.

"Mr. Watkins," said the friendliest voice Joe had ever heard. "This is Gabby from the Second Chance Temp Agency."

"Have you called here before? I think I may have

gotten a phone message." Is that why that post-it note had ended up on his desk?

"No, Mr. Watkins. This is my first and only call." Her voice was like pure cane sugar. He was getting a cavity just listening to her. "I'm calling to remind you of your nine am appointment tomorrow."

"Sorry, Gabby was it? I don't recall ever—" He did not get a chance to finish.

"We will send a car to pick you up in the morning at eight thirty-six which will get you here with about ten minutes to spare. See you in the morning, Mr. Watkins." Then she hung up.

Joe left feeling almost drunk with all the events that had occurred. After a night's sleep it hadn't worn off yet. He woke up this morning feeling just as muddled. He gets up, gets dressed, and gets outside to wait for the car, and his future to arrive.

CHAPTER SEVEN

On the elevator headed down to the lobby I pull myself together. *I can do this. The only way to get Deedy back into my life is to finish this assignment.* I ignore the overwhelming sense of emptiness that I am feeling right now, and replace it with a new sense of responsibility. I have to watch over Joe. Make sure he safely returns back to himself and to his family and friends. That thought is suitably renewing, and I find myself getting downright excited.

When I get down to the lobby the elevator does not just stop. Instead, it halts, goes a bit, then squeals. The lights flicker before they go out completely, and the doors open just enough for me to see that I am in fact on the bottom floor. I have to pry the doors open the rest of the way. *Pretty shoddy mechanics for paradise.* I think before I see it sitting on the floor next to a potted plant. It seems to be a tool belt, complete with very unfamiliar objects hanging from it that I can only assume are tools. The funny thing about the belt is what is written across it. PATTERSON ELEVATOR REPAIRS, it says right across the front. Ha! I am laughing out loud at the prospect of me repairing anything. I mean, seriously, I once abandoned a 1994 Plymouth Duster on the side of the highway because the engine light came on. Well, that and that car never had an ounce of style. Oh, and there was the time when Bobby was away, working as a manager of a carnival, and I had to throw away a sink full of dishes because the dishwasher started to smoke and make the kitchen smell all like an electrical fire. Yes, I realize that I could have washed the dishes by hand, but that would be in direct conflict with my natural tendency to be lazy. Plus the aforementioned smoky smell in the kitchen. I ate out for the next five weeks until Bobby came home. Suffice it to say, there is no way in Heaven or Hell that I have the talent or inclination to fix this elevator. They might as well have left me a table of scalpels and a belt that says PATTERSON BRAIN SURGERY across the front of it. Hopefully, this is part of Deedy's magic, otherwise Joe is never going to get up to the thirty-seventh floor in time to please Gabby.

I pull on the tool belt and think to myself here goes nothing' as I manage to pry off the small plated cover directly under the buttons. Under my breath I start doing my best Scotty impression, a real homage to Star Trek. "Ay Cap't, I don't know why the turbo lift is fucking up. Maybe it's because we are about twenty minutes into the episode, and that is always when it happens?"

My reverie gets interrupted by the arrival of a young looking, quite handsome man. Young, but rugged. His face is creased by a permanent frown. He is average height but has a stocky build, as though he has spent most of his living years sustained on take out, junk food, and the empty calories of a six-pack every night. He has deep, expressive brown eyes that are now looking at me with a question still beginning to form within them. I suddenly realize that he may have already asked his question, but I haven't heard him because I was busy monologuing to myself in my imaginary spaceship.

"Sorry," I say. "I don't know if you just asked me something or not, and if you did…well, I'm going to need you to repeat it." Then, very lamely I add, "You know, concentrating on the elevator and all." I feel a blush rising in my face.

"That's okay," he says quickly. "I didn't mean to interrupt your work. I'm just not exactly sure where I am supposed to be." His voice is deep and silky smooth, like the announcer in a coffee commercial. "I have an interview at a place called Second Chance? I think it's a temp agency. All I have is this post-it note." He hands it to me with a look of desperation. I don't even read it. I have seen about forty of those in my afterlife, including the one I found that brought me here the first time.

"Sure!" I say, getting up and brushing myself off as if I've been doing anything besides staring blankly at a bunch of wires and mumbling to myself in a bad Scottish accent. "You must be Joe Watkins." I hold out a hand to shake his.

"Yes…yes, that's me." His surprise is evident. He clasps my hand too with equal surprise. There isn't a lot of touching in Hell. And of course, what he doesn't know is that there also is absolutely no touching in Deedy's world until it's time to make him see. That won't happen until my job is done. So I had better get on it.

"No worries, Joe, step on in, and I'll get you up there in plenty of time. My name is Louise, by the way."

"Thanks, Louise," he says, stepping in and looking around. "Are you sure this thing won't trap us between floors during a raging battle with the Klingons?" He looks at me and smiles.

"Damn, you heard that," I say with my own smile. "And you are already making fun of me. Which means you will fit in around here with no problem."

"Sorry, didn't mean to eavesdrop. I just couldn't help myself. I was a Trekkie too." He seems like a very warm guy. I get excited again about the prospect of seeing him through the next few weeks.

"In that case, prepare for take-off, Captain!" I say as I push the button with the number thirty-seven on it. I quickly cross my fingers and send a wish up to Gabby that this elevator is miraculously fixed as it does come to life and start to climb. Joe seems to notice that we are heading up and suddenly seems nervous.

I try to comfort him. "I know it's up there. I freaked out the first time, but you will get used to it." I laugh as I remember crawling on the floor as if the whole building was going to give way and I would fall to another death.

"No, I'll be fine with the height. I'm just worried about the interview. I assume you know the folks I have to talk to up there? I mean, since you knew my name and all…"

"Sure, everyone around here knows Gabby," I say, then pause, trying not to choke on my next words. "And of course, the boss." *Hold it together, Louise.*

"Anything I need to know? I really need a job, as you know. And the only thing I have ever done as an adult, both living and dead is being a reporter. So there is not much that I bring to the table." He gets kind of misty, like he is in mourning.

"Just be yourself, Joe. Believe me, you already have everything you need. You will be fine," I say as the doors open up to the lobby of the agency. As soon as Joe steps out I start to lean on the close door button. I can't breathe as I wait for the doors to begin to shut. I can hear Gabby's voice offering Joe a cup of her wonderful coffee. I strain to hear Deedy's voice boom through the corridor, but there is nothing but silence and the emptiness fills me once again. As the doors finally draw together and I am finally headed down, I sink to the floor of the elevator and start to sob again.

I pull myself together and realize I have nothing to do for the hour or so that it will take Joe to get grilled for the first time in Deedy's office. So I sit on the curb and look around with my new eyes. Better said, I guess it would be my old eyes. Everything is back to orange, and it's all drab and depressing again. I can no longer see the beautiful sky or any of the heavenly creatures that fill it.

The tears are now falling silently, but they are still with me.

This would be the perfect time for a cigarette. My mind wanders back to that same old thought. This is about the millionth time I have longed for a smoke since dying. You can't get smokes in Hell, and while you can in Heaven, and many do, I absolutely refuse to go back to smoking. I quit when I found out I was pregnant with my daughter, who I named after Linda but we called her Dinny. Of course, soon after that I was dying of cancer. And after that, I spent thirty some years in a place where you constantly feel like your lungs, along with the rest of you, could burst into flames at any moment. You can see how the whole romance with cigarettes can lose its luster. And while I am adamant that I will never be a smoker again, that doesn't mean that occasionally I miss it. I miss the ritual, the slight pull when you remove the first cigarette in the pack, the feel of it between your fingers, the kiss between breath and fire by a single tether between your lips, the first delicious draw, the feeling inside your body as you fill it with smoke like the ambient light of a firefly in a jar, and finally the lovely fog that surrounds you as you exhale. I can practically see the smoke now. No, wait, I actually can see the smoke. I let my eyes follow the creamy air to its source.

Standing in front of me is the single most fabulous looking man, no…person, I have ever laid eyes on. He is tall, about six feet one inch, blond hair with gorgeous eyes the color of wheat. His skin is bronzed by a sun that no longer shines on any of us here. His T-shirt and blue jeans hang from his body as though he has been created wearing them. And while his outfit is modest and covers him completely, it gives enough hints as to the perfect body underneath that I find myself a bit breathless.

"I thought I was blind to everyone from Heaven," I

say, suddenly glad I'm sitting down, afraid my knees would buckle underneath me if I were standing.

"And so you are. Cigarette?" His voice is as beautiful as the mouth from which his words have just escaped. His accent is English. Posh and very sexy.

"You can't be a Hellion. Not with those clothes, and smokes, and stuff," I say, like a little know-it-all.

"If you insist, Ms. Louise Patterson," he says with a cool smile that reveals stunningly white teeth, all perfect and straight.

"Not fair! How can you get to know my name if I can't know yours?"

"Because of what I understand of you, Ms. Sweetness and Light, you tend to go more for the mysterious type."

Now, I have to say for all the years I have been dead, in both Heaven and Hell, I have never been hit on. Not even once. And don't get me wrong, it's not that I'm unattractive. In fact, in life I was kind of hot in my own way. I was used to every kind of guy, from the tight ass banker to the scumbag who was about to mug the tight ass banker on the street, hitting on me. But in Hell, no one cares to hit on anyone because sex is not a possibility, and romance is even less of an option. And in Heaven, no one hits on anyone because, to be honest, as great as sex and dating and romance is, it has nothing compared to the bliss of Paradise.

That is why tall, dark, and mysterious just threw me. Threw me enough that I actually ask, "Did you just hit on me?" It is out of my mouth before my brain even knows it is about to leave.

He throws back his head and laughs uproariously. *What am I, doing stand-up comedy here?* Then he takes out a cigarette, puts it in the front pocket of my denim shirt, and walks away. He waves without looking back, as if he knows that I am staring at him walk away.

"Great. I've been back here for less than a day and this horrible place is already fucking with me. Welcome home, Louise!" I say, just as Joe walks through the door and onto the street.

◄

CHAPTER EIGHT

Linda was kind of proud of the fact that she had never learned to type. Not even when everyone got computers and the internet and the average kid could type seventy words per minute before they could eat solid food. She had only worked for a few years before marrying Hank. Always as a hostess in a restaurant, or a "Can I get that in your size?" girl in a retail store. With all of that in mind, her first day as a legal secretary did not hold a lot of promise.

Until she actually walks into the offices of Davis, Morgan, and Lugner, the largest law firm in Hell as far as she could tell. Behind the desk at the entrance is the woman who has interviewed her yesterday. She smiles to herself as she remembers the so-called interview. It basically went like this:

Linda walks in and states that she is looking for a job.

This very crabby woman looks at her through teeny tiny slits of eyes and says, "Have you ever worked in a law office?"

Linda says, "No."

"Do you have any secretarial skills?"

Linda says, "No."

"Nothing? No typing, no dictation, no phone étiquette?"

Linda says, "No."

"Would you consider yourself a people person?"

Linda stops and thinks about it. After ninety years of dealing with just a handful of folks, many of whom she was related to or thought of as family, she still ended up taking out the one that was supposed to be her favorite before shuffling off the mortal coil. So ultimately she gave the only answer she could. "No."

"Okay, you start tomorrow. Nine am," says Ms. Grumpy Pants, then goes back to doing whatever it was she was doing, which by Linda's best guess is pretty much pretending Linda doesn't exist. So she turns around, walks out the door, and leaves. Officially an employee!

Now, Linda is awake and ready for her new career. She notices that the closet once again has a single outfit hanging inside. *Ah,* she thinks to herself, *the magical world of Hell.* She notices that this particular piece of magic is a skin tight pencil skirt dress with a print that she is having difficulty looking at directly. This dress pulled over her aged body, with all its lumps and bumps really should come with a warning label that reads "May cause epileptic seizures." Not to mention actually trying to move or walk in this skirt will be downright comical. Her thoughts land on an old memory of a character on the Carol Burnett show. Mrs. Wiggins, a ditzy secretary who inches along like a penguin walking with an egg between her legs. *Unfortunately, I have neither the figure nor the comic timing of Carol.* Linda thinks with a sigh.

Setting off on the somewhat short—today is a bit longer, due to the skirt—walk to her new office, Linda begins to wonder about the nature of her job. Why do we need a law office in Hell? To sue people? Can you sue someone for screwing you over in a place where virtually everyone has screwed someone over? And what do you sue for? A million dollars? Why the fuck would you even need a million dollars here? So you could buy the biggest house or the nicest car in the grandest shithole in the universe? She starts to actually laugh at the absurdity of that idea. Perhaps she will have the chance to ask Ms. Frowny Face during orientation or whatever. But Linda is also a bit doubtful. She has found pretty consistently since arriving here that no one is forthcoming with information, and certainly not up for friendly conversation either.

When she walks into Davis, Morgan, and Lugner her doubts are confirmed. No one greets her, welcomes her, or tells her what to do. *So much for orientation.* Linda thinks as she wanders through the office.

"Hello? I'm supposed to start working here today!" She yells to no in particular.

"Well then, I suggest you get started." Ms. Sourpuss is back. She reaches over and grabs a pile of manila folders which she then drops in front of Linda. "Here. File."

What was I thinking, of course was *there's an orientation, and apparently that was just it.* She looks at the dour woman in front of her and says, "Where?"

The woman just turns and with a sigh of exasperation walks away, leaving Linda standing there holding a manila folder with no idea what to do with it. So she just opens up a drawer and tosses it in. Then she grabs another and tosses that one in. Then she walks across the room, opens up another random drawer and tosses a bunch more in.

At one point this very small, yet incredibly fat man walks in and straight through the office where he then just seems to disappear. She assumes by his gait and general demeanor that this must be Mr. Davis, Mr. Morgan, or Mr. Lugner. Linda remembers a joke. This woman gets called for jury duty and while the Judge is questioning her, she says, "I should not be on this jury." The Judge of course asks her why, and she says, "Because I knew the second I laid eyes on his shifty face, his shiny suit, and his cheesy smile that he was guilty as sin!" The Judge says, "Ma'am. Sit down and prepare to hear testimony. That man you are referring to is the prosecutor."

She laughs to herself as she continues to approach this exercise in futility.

Once she realizes that if she keeps up this pace all day she will be out of manila folders way before she's out of work day, Linda gets the bright idea to take a break. She goes in search of a break room. This is a law office, they must have a break room, or a kitchen.

She walks down a hall and the smell hits her before the room even comes into her immediate sight. When it does she realizes she is looking at the most disgusting kitchen in the entire universe. She looks around from one vile table to the next. Once she crosses the threshold her eyes begin to water from the stench. Linda is unaware of whether or not there are rats in the afterlife, but if there are even they would not hang out in this kitchen. This kitchen would probably make Gordon Ramsey burst into tears and run to his mother so that she could rock him to sleep.

There probably is no food or drink in this establishment with an expiration date before 1937, but even if there was, Linda was not going to eat or drink anything until this kitchen is presentable. *And,* she thinks to herself, *this will make the day go by a lot faster.*

So she takes a deep breath, decides breathing is totally unnecessary in the afterlife, and dives in. After about an hour, there is something kitchen shaped starting to emerge. After another hour and a half, things are actually starting to gleam. Which is pretty damn impressive considering the only cleaning product Linda could find was an ancient can of Comet that had fossilized and was now more brick like than cleaning powder. When she's finally done, she stands back and admires her own handiwork. Miss Meany strides by and stops dead in her tracks.

"What do you think you are doing in here?" She glances around with an expression that makes it seem like Linda has made the kitchen worse.

"I spiffed up the kitchen!" Linda says brightly. For some reason "spiffing up the kitchen" seems a little more diplomatic than "shoveling out this enormous shithole."

"Well, Ms. Spiffer, I think you just cleaned out your future at Davis, Morgan, and Lugner!" Then she turns on her heel and storms out.

Linda is dazed. Her future at Davis, Morgan, and Lugner? What could they fire her for? All she did was clean the kitchen. She walks back out to the office and sees that her pile of Manila folders have grown. Is that what she was so upset over? Linda shirking her important "tossing files around the room aimlessly" duties?

Suddenly the small fat man emerges from his office and bellows, "Mrs. Miller, in my office immediately!"

Linda walks into his office like a prisoner approaching the electric chair. Miss Meany is also in there and pipes in as soon as Linda is safely enclosed behind the shut door. "Mr. Davis, I had no idea what she was doing, or even where she had gone for three hours. I assumed she was hiding in the bathroom or something like a normal person would do on their first day."

"A normal person would hide in the bathroom for three hours?" Linda questions.

"Regardless," Mr. Davis says brusquely, "we can't have people making our workplace nicer. Now that kitchen is an amenity. Do you have any idea how vulnerable that makes us?" Apparently, he's talking to Linda.

"I'm sorry, I'm new," Linda says, suddenly feeling like she's on a lost episode of The Twilight Zone.

"Well, I hope you'll take this experience as a learning experience. You will not be cleaning any kitchens at your next job." Mr. Davis seems pretty determined. He reaches in his desk and pulls out a pink slip.

"Mr. Davis, if I can just explain my actions." Linda is

desperate. She can't lose her job on the first day.

"There is no explanation for such heinous behavior." Miss Meany chips in with her two cents.

"Excuse me? It's not like I set fire to the office. Although I'm not sure that wouldn't have earned me a promotion." Linda has decided that she hates this woman.

"Obviously you just have not gotten acclimated—" Meany is interrupted by the phone on Mr. Davis desk.

Mr. Davis answers, "Hello, Davis here…oh hey…yes…yes…but you understand that she cleaned the kitchen…no, she actually made the appliances shine…yes…Alright all right…I understand…goodbye." Mr. Davis hangs up.

"Who was that? And why were you talking about me?" Linda says questioningly.

"What makes you think he was discussing you?" Meany says.

"Because he said 'she cleaned the kitchen.' If he had said 'yes, she still has a giant oak crammed directly up her ass' I would have assumed he was talking about you." Linda is getting more acclimated by the minute.

Mr. Davis stands and grabs the pink slip. He rips it in two and tosses it in the nearest trash can. "Mrs. Miller, you may return to your filing."

"I don't understand! You were going to fire her!" Miss Meany's day just went south.

"And now I'm not," Mr. Davis says. Then he leans over and says much quieter, "Lugner's orders."

Miss Meany stiffens and looks over at Linda. "So, get back to work. Those files aren't going to file themselves." And she stalks out of the office.

Linda doesn't know whether to feel relieved or not. It's a crappy job, but it is a job. Linda guesses that since Mr. Lugner made the call, that means Mr. Davis may be a partner in name only. Lugner seems to be the boss.

"Thank you, Mr. Davis," she says quietly and goes back to work. After a few more hours, it is as though nothing happened. Linda is back to *persona non grata.*

Suddenly, as she is throwing another folder in a drawer, she flashes on a needlepoint placard that hung in her own mother's house her entire childhood. That placard said, in tall, graceful lettering, "Today is the first day of the rest of your life." The idea of eternity falls on Linda like an anvil. This is now her life, and her life is now forever and ever. Infinite and unending, there is no spaghetti sauce that she can make that would ever get her out of this one.

The only upside to having this miserable job is that absolutely no one is paying attention to her. No one sees her take the rest of the pile and throw it behind a filing cabinet. No one notices when she finds a corner, sits down on the floor, and starts to sob.

CHAPTER NINE

Joe walks by me just as I am finishing up my "Welcome Home" spiel to now no one. "So I guess you caught me talking to myself, again," I say, embarrassed.

"Who, me? I don't know what you're talking about," he says, smiling at me devilishly. I start to walk, matching my steps with his, and we begin an easy conversation. Well, at least to him it probably seemed easy.

"So, what did you think of Deedy?" I asked, not at all sounding like a teenage girl passing notes to her bestie during math class. At least I hope I don't.

"Amazingly cool man," he says, his respect evident.

"Was he wearing one of his designer suits? Those suits make me drool. Literally. I have to ask Gabby for a tissue before going into his office." I try to sound casual and funny, like there isn't a giant boulder now forming in my throat.

"A suit? No. He was dressed very casually actually, khaki pants and a polo shirt. I mean, it was a nice polo shirt and pants. Of course, Kmart probably looks like Gucci to me after very many years here. I asked him where he found his clothes, and I admitted to him, practically a stranger that I was more than a little jealous, but he just seemed to brush it off. He also seems to have a problem touching anybody. He wouldn't shake my hand. Is that weird? I thought it was kind of weird. Is it weird that I'm gushing this much over another man?" Now he looks at me nervously.

Internally I breathe a sigh of relief at the thought of something familiar regarding Deedy, and I laugh at Joe. "Yep, that's our Deedy. He can be a strange one at first, but don't worry, you'll get used to it. You seem like a great guy," and then I add quickly, "and a very normal guy."

"He reminds me of my grandfather. Kindly old man with that Midwestern accent."

Kindly old man? Midwestern accent? What is Joe talking about? Then I start to smile a bit, because I realize that Deedy is not appearing to Joe the same way he appears to me. "Yeah, a great guy." I repeat, trying not to let Joe know about the sudden tears welling up in my eyes. I say simply, "That is very, very true." I have to shake this off or I'm going to melt down again and he will think I'm some kind of nut job.

"So, let's talk about you!" I say, surprised by my own bright, suddenly happy sounding voice. "Where are we going?"

"Well," he says, looking at me with just a hint of suspicion. "I'm headed to a greasy spoon diner where I get to start my glorious new career as a short order cook. Keep in mind that I have never even boiled water, I don't think, and I'm pretty sure I would remember if I had ever made a gourmet meal or even anything other than a fucking sandwich in my life. So this will be quite an adventure." He's laughing at himself now.

"Let me just say, it sounds to me like you are absolutely perfect to be a cook in Hell. You did realize after all this time that opposing skill sets are a plus down here, right?"

"Well, then you are absolutely correct. I am going to be an amazing short order cook in Hell," Joe replies with a slight smile.

When we get to the diner, I shake his hand and wish him luck, then walk on wondering if I should come back later to check on him or go see Hank. I could go check with Gabby, of course, but that means going back to that literally God forsaken office. Well, technically, the office isn't God forsaken. I am. I decide that before I go back I'll do a little sightseeing in the old neighborhood. Hell and Heaven occupy the same space, so it is not like I never see any part of my old life in my new one. For instance, I walk past IB&FW every day, but I haven't seen my apartment in years. Part of that is magic. Each residential side has their own limits to vision that keep the other side blind. I have decided while I can now see all things Hellcentric, I miss my Heaven eyes. I walk down the street and memories flood over me. Even smells and sounds are crowding into my brain, each demanding their own table front and center for the cabaret. When I get to my old building, I back up and look into the window of my old apartment. It seems like nothing has changed. Same gray walls, same colorless furniture barely able to stand alone let alone offer comfort to anyone using it. I close my eyes and imagine myself back there.

I think about the woman who used to sit up there and dream and cry and suffer and remember. I think about the girl who had resigned herself to this eternity, not daring to imagine another place, a Heaven in which redemption and forgiveness could be a part of my future. And then I think about Joe, who is at the beginning of his great final destiny. He still has the further realizations about Deedy and Gabby and Paradise. And most importantly, he still gets to find out about himself. That he is Forgiven. That he is Loved.

In a lot of ways this part of our personal eternal journey is the best. Because whether you're in Heaven or in Hell, it is what it is. There is no growth, or change or epiphanies about life. Life is now over and all that's left is consequence without action. Human experience is now behind all of us until those of us who believe that we are damned come into this time of transition. Then we get to grow more than adolescence, motherhood, and middle age all put together. I feel another pang of envy for Joe who is just starting, and another ache of homesickness for Deedy's love.

"Okay," I say to myself as I get up and walk purposefully back toward the agency, "I'm done being a fucking whiner." This little roll down memory lane has renewed my sensibilities. I can see now that this is temporary and not about me. This is for Joe and Linda, and I will be home soon. Now I have to hike up my big girl panties and get back to work.

I begin walking more quickly. Now without fear, but instead with a slight amusement.

When I was alive, I rarely even thought about God. Oh, at various times in my past I said desperate prayers to anyone up there who may be listening. Praying for stupid things like 'Please don't let me pregnant' or 'Please let me pass that math test' or 'Please let me stop puking and I swear I'll never drink again'! And if anyone ever asked me if 'do you believe in God', of course my answer would be 'Yes, definitely.' But to actually spend time thinking about the fact that there was a God, or building a relationship with my creator? No.

Then for my first twenty odd years in death, I was completely devoid of God's presence, but I didn't miss it because I didn't realize anything was missing. Now after just a very few years of having a real one-on-one with the big guy, I'm rendered inconsolable because I can't see or feel him. Ain't that a kick in the teeth!

I walk into the agency, and Gabby looks at me with relief. "Lou! It's good to see you. I thought for a minute or two that you were avoiding me."

"I was," I say with total honesty. I have found that to be the best tactic with her, since she could tell if I was lying anyway. "But don't take it personally. It was more about not being able to see Deedy than seeing you, if you understand."

"Of course, how are you making out?"

"Good. Joe is at work, and I was wondering if it is okay if I go hang with Hank for a while. What do you think?"

"I think that is a great idea," she says warmly. "If Joe should need you, I'll get in touch."

I pause before I go and after a brief moment of hesitation I say, "So, I met a man."

"What man?" she asks. Is that alarm in her eyes?

"I don't know his name. He wouldn't tell me. But he offered me a cigarette, and he was dressed impeccably, so I assume he's a Heaven resident. Right?"

"I guess. You didn't take it, right?" All of the sudden she's turned into my big sister.

"Of course not. That really isn't the point."

"Sorry, what is?"

"How can I see him?"

"I don't know. I don't know who he is, and quite frankly I haven't been paying that much attention to you, I've been more centered on Joe."

"Of course you have. Sorry," I say sheepishly. However, I can't help but notice that her smile seems forced. I think she's lying to me. See? That is why I need some super powers. So that I will know for a fact when I am getting snowed by an archangel.

"My only advice is to stop paying attention to well-dressed cigarette pushers and keep your eye on your assignment," Gabby says jokingly.

"I will. I actually like Joe. He seems very nice." And I mean that. He really is a fabulous guy. "I will be here tomorrow to take Joe to his new assignment. Can I get a hint as to what it is?" I say with conspiracy in my voice.

"Actually, I think you'll be taking him to the same one. It doesn't look like he's getting fired today."

"What? How does that happen?"

"Every journey is different, Lou. Some people actually do know how to keep a job longer than a few hours." Now she's smiling genuinely. Actually, now I'm being mocked by an archangel.

"You know, for a benevolent heavenly being you sure know how to kick a girl when she's down," I say. I'm teasing. Kind of.

"I am glad you're enjoying the assignment. And you seem to be doing well so far. Now go see Hank." Gabby gives me a big smile and sets me on my way.

On the way to Hank's I feel a little bewildered. What does Gabby know about the gorgeous stranger who injected himself into my life today? And why wouldn't she tell me about him, if she does know something?

Oh, and don't even get me started on Joe keeping his job. I really am trying not to get a case of the ass over that, but seriously? Do I hold some kind of record as the biggest fuck up ever in the history of Second Chance Temp Agency?

Hell has a ton of torments, and there's a new one every day. But some never change. I feel as confused and alone as I did when I first arrived here.

I'm looking forward to spending time with Hank. Not just to help him understand, but perhaps to soak up a little understanding for myself as well.

Hank was just as happy to see me as he had been last night at his welcoming party.

"Lou! So happy you are here! Come in. What can I get you?"

"You've already stocked up on groceries?" I am surprised.

"The Loft came stocked! Even the refrigerator was full. How's that, me living in a loft. I feel all fancy and big citified." Hank's enthusiasm is contagious.

"Did it come with soda?" I say.

"Yep. Crushed ice or cubed? Go figure! Two kinds of ice!" Hank goes to the kitchen, guffawing over his ice bounty. He brings me my soda, and we sit down.

"How was your day? Your new assignment working out?" he asks. "Do you know when I'll get an assignment? I really feel like I should become a productive member of society. And with all this new found energy I really want to be working. I imagine there is probably some really great jobs up here. Will they give me choices or will they just know what it is I'm supposed to do?"

I start to laugh. "Whoa! Slow down there, Mr. French! There is plenty of time for you to think about what you want to do up here. In fact, there is nothing but time. Or better said, there is no such thing as time. Well, that's not right either. I dunno. Eternity still gives me a headache. And yes, thank you, my new assignment is great so far. But I'm way more interested in you." I say, "Tell me how it's been since you got here? I mean, aside from the burning desire to join the labor force."

"It has been amazing. Getting to see people that I have missed so much. It really is overwhelming. I just wish Linda was here," he says with a tinge of sadness.

"That's what I want to talk to you about," I say, still processing hearing Linda's name said out loud. "Do you remember how you died?"

"Of course," he answers. "That would be a tough thing to forget."

"So has anybody explained to you how things work? Like how it is decided whether you go to Heaven or Hell?" I ask him nervously.

"No. In fact, no one has mentioned Hell. It's like they're afraid to say the word because they think I don't know. But of course I do. When I got here they showed me the remote viewing screens, so I was aware that she was dead too. And when she wasn't here, I assume she was lost or she was going to Hell. I was told that she had died at the same time and the same way I did. It really didn't take a rocket scientist." He seems agitated.

"Well, I guess I am here to answer any questions you may have," I say with caution.

"Here's what I wanna know. How does she deserve eternal damnation for one act? Especially since I've already forgiven her and I'm the one she murdered, right? Shouldn't that count for something?"

"Really?" I ask him. "You have already forgiven her?"

"I'm pretty sure I forgave her the second I realized what she was doing," he says, laughing again like we were back on the ice or the loft conversation.

I, on the other hand, start blubbering almost immediately. "Hank." Is all I can say. I sink back in my chair as he continues.

"I have always known that Linda was too good for me. She was a gift, something sent to me that I didn't deserve."

"I think you are selling yourself short." I choke on a small sob.

"Please. You of all people, Louise, were standing in line to make sure I knew that."

"Oh, Hank." Now my tears are falling freely.

"That toast at our rehearsal dinner." His voice is not accusing. It was just a statement.

"That toast was totally inappropriate." I am suddenly filled with regret.

"That toast was truth," he says.

My head betrays me, and my brain flees to the past to recall that horrible night one more time. That speech. That drunken, stupid, arrogant speech.

"Would you like to know the secret of the universe, kids? Cuz I've got it right here. Men always want what they can't have, and never want what they've got. And women always want what they used to have and they will settle for anything or anyone that gives them the illusion that they can have it back. And there will be moments, and this might actually be one for our Linda, when you can actually sit back and say that you are content, almost happy with your life, with yourself and the one standing next to you...and you should embrace those moments, because they will all go away—quickly."

Fresh, new tears are now flowing. "There was nothing true about anything I said that day."

"Except that happiness is fleeting. Maybe not for all the reasons you listed in your rant, but even that is sort of true. Happiness doesn't last because if you are happy every single day, it starts to feel normal. Then you take it for granted. And I can now tell you that if love is taken for granted long enough, it becomes something else."

"All right, I know this sounds bizarre. But I don't think Linda stopped loving you."

"I will concede that she probably didn't realize it. We had been together so long, we learned every pet peeve, so we could avoid annoying one another. We learned each other's favorite things, so we always knew what to do or get for each other. After years and years of that we had nothing to fight about, but we also had nothing new to offer one another. To be honest, by the end we were barely seeing each other." Now Hank is crying too.

"Hank, I love Linda, you know I do. But you can't take any responsibility for what she did."

Hank looks at me and gives me a weak smile. "Lou, you have been dead for a long time, a lot longer than I have to be certain. But I have the advantage. I have lived a lot longer than you. Take it from an old man, Linda made that choice all on her own. But the darkness that allowed her to make it so blindly? I have to be able to admit that I created it. Inadvertently, with neglect not malice, but it was me."

I just look at him. "Oh, Hank," is all I can say, once again. I get up and wrap my arms around his neck. "I am so sorry. Sorry this happened to you and to Linda."

"Don't be sorry for me. Look where I am. But Linda. Poor Linda." He embraces me back.

"You don't know, do you?" I look at him curiously. "No one has told you?"

"Told me what?"

I sit back down. "I apologize in advance. This is not going to be short." And I begin to tell my story. The tale of my afterlife. About how after I died there was no party or welcoming, just waking up in excruciating heat and orange light. How I got a job at IP&FW and worked there for dozens of years until the day I found Deedy's temp agency. Well, until Deedy found me, to be more precise.

Hank was suitably enthralled. He found my misadventures from being a short lived garbage collector, taxi driver, and beautician hilarious. He took comfort from the fact that in Hell you can't remember a lot about your life, and each of those jobs were designed to force me to remember the good in mine, and the good in me. When I tell him about my final job, at a day care center, about children in Hell and what they really are, he looks concerned. His concern turns to fear as I relay my experience there.

"Those little bastards tore me to pieces. But that was what it took to make me remember Dinny. That was pretty much my ticket to Heaven."

"So what you are saying is Linda has a chance at this?"

"Of course she does. It may take some time, but

remember what I was trying to say about time earlier? At some point Linda will be joining you here." I decide to leave it at that for now. I choose not to tell him about my new assignment or why I asked for it. I get the feeling that he may not be able to wrap his head around all that right now. So I end the story with only half of it told.

His gratitude however, is complete. He draws me into another bear hug, and we hold each other like dear old friends.

"You know, I think we would have been much closer in life if I had lived long enough," I say.

"Well, now we have eternity, right? Thank you for everything, Louise. From the time I got here until tonight."

We say our goodbyes, and I am actually looking forward to getting home. It has been a long, weird day. I open up my door and walk into my apartment and realize that it's not over yet. Seems I need one more surprise.

My apartment is exactly like I left it this morning. Except it is completely empty. No comfy couch, no soothing fireplace, no huge bed with a mattress that I can sink into. I start looking through closets and find a cot that I set up and fall into. I seriously consider getting on my knees next to it, but I know I would be talking into a void. Instead, I lie back and try to sleep. *Just another wonderful day in Hell.* I think as I drift off to dreamless slumber.

CHAPTER TEN

Joe gets up and walks to his closet with the reckless abandon of a long-term resident of Hell. He puts on what looks like pirates britches. He actually wishes he had a mirror so he could check himself out. For the top it's one of those turtleneck sweaters that spies always wore in the movies in the 60s. Since Joe is pretty sure he remembers when these were actually in style, it doesn't seem that bad. Until he gets it on. Then he gets the cosmic joke. When it's blazing hot outside and you are wearing a turtleneck, you might as well just walk around with a giant chain around your neck slowly strangling you all day.

"What a perfect outfit to endure overwhelming heat, standing over a grill filled with disgusting food, and of course heavy grease seeping into the fabric to make it even more uncomfortable. Not to mention smellier." Yes, Joe has a tendency to talk to himself first thing in the morning. He then starts to hum 'Oh, What a Beautiful Morning' with as much sarcasm as
one can muster while humming.

Today is his fourth day as a short order cook at the diner. He royally sucks at it, which seems to be exactly what they are looking for in a cook. Stan, his boss—who prefers to be called Captain for some probably documentably crazy reason—seems very pleased by his work. This mildly disturbs Joe, since his record thus far is two out of five meals coming back. And people in Hell aren't polite in good conditions. When they send food back at a restaurant that if it were in the land of the living Zagat wouldn't even allow their guide to be read within a mile of the property, they tend to do it with a sort of profane flair that sticks with you long after it's been delivered. Kind of like the grease. The remaining three customers also returned their meals, in a very different way. Yes, sixty percent of the people who ate Joe's food *barfed*. Not to mention he has set the kitchen on fire twice. He has a theory that the only reason they still have customers is because people get a sense of entertainment watching him make an ass of himself.

He walks out the door and is pleased because he got out of the house a half hour early. He just sort of wants to walk to work alone today. It is not like he doesn't like Louise, or that he isn't very appreciative of her help since he started at the agency. She's just a little odd and incredibly talkative. And kind of stalkerish. Every day she is waiting for him outside of his apartment and walks him to work. And for some reason, she seems irritated that he has not gotten fired yet, which he finds disconcerting. So, every morning he finds himself having to make conversation with a woman who is a stranger, and seems irritated at him. Joe is a reporter at his core, and he made a living observing people and situations. And his gut tells him that this sudden friendship with Louise is not really genuine. It has set-up written all over it. She works for Deedy, and for some reason Deedy wants him watched. Louise pretends to like Joe so she can keep tabs on him.

He really wants to confront Deedy, but Deedy makes him nervous. Not nervous like "palm sweaty," "heart beating" nervous, but more like "really wants his approval" kind of nervous. Joe still doesn't understand why Deedy is so different than anyone else in Hell. The clothes, the office, those incredible chairs. And Gabby with her root beer that is ice cold like he used to drink when he was a kid. Why would a man like that have someone spying on someone like Joe? And why does that bring Joe a sense of comfort? But as nice as it seems, it is also nice just to have some time to process his thoughts and to prepare for another shitty day without Louise yammering at him.

When Joe enters the diner, Stan the Captain glances at the clock and starts in on him. "What's up with the early bird routine? You trying for employee of the month?" He says in his usual gruff way.

"Why would I possibly assume that arriving early would earn me such a position of honor?"

"Like we even have an employee of the month. Here's your apron." Stan tosses a once white apron across the room to Joe. "Get to prepping for the breakfast crowd. I'll be in the back." Stan starts back to the kitchen.

"My last name is spelled W-A-T-K-I-N-S," Joe yells after him. "You know, for the plaque."

"I'll write that down as soon as I let go of my sides from laughing," Stan yells back, with no laughter anywhere in his tone.

Joe has tied on his apron and is currently pouring himself a cup of the swill this place insists on calling coffee, when he hears the first customer of the day come in. He turns around and sees a girl. She looks young, mousy brown hair, a look of confusion and terror in her eyes. She sits at the counter and looks at the menu in a stand-up plastic holder that makes it handy to order from when you are sitting at the counter. She seems to panic as she sets it back down and starts to weep.

Newbie, Joe thinks instantly.

"Can I get you something?" Joe asks, not trying to sound too friendly.

"No, I'm fine." The girl looks around as if she is still trying to determine whether this is a nightmare or not.

Joe sighs. "How long have you been here?"

"I don't know. An hour? A day? A week?" The desperation in her voice is thicker than pancake syrup.

Pancake syrup anywhere but here, where it's the consistency of play-doh and smells of feet.

Joe is struck by this poor girl. He stops to wonder what someone who looks so innocent could possibly have done to end up here. Of course, after all this time he knows better than to be swayed by helplessness or beauty. But she is beautiful. Her eyes so big and blue, and her hair falls across her shoulders in soft curls. Joe wants to help her, but how do you help someone who suddenly finds themselves in eternal despair? He turns around and grabs a mug. Suddenly, he is filled with inspiration. He takes the mug back to the kitchen and grabs a saucepan. He goes to the stove and is surprised to find that all the ingredients he wants are right there. He starts making his concoction like he was channeling Julia Childs. He is suddenly possessed with the idea of making the most delicious cup of hot cocoa ever made in Hell. He puts in cream, cocoa powder, and sugar. At the end he grabs some chili powder from the spice rack and puts that in too along with a pinch of salt. He tastes it and is actually surprised with his own talent. He cannot recall ever making anything, let alone homemade hot chocolate with chili. The taste explodes in his mouth, but slides smoothly down his throat. He pours it in the mug and takes it to the girl.

"Oh, I can't," she says, dismissing it immediately.

"My treat," he says, pushing the steaming mug toward her.

She picks up the mug and breaths in the steam before she takes a sip. Then her eyes register real surprise as she looks up at him.

"You put chili in here!" she exclaims. "How did you know?"

"Know what?" Joe is bewildered but pleased as he watches her take another long draw from her mug.

When she is done, she wipes her mouth with the back of her hand in a gesture that makes her appear both childlike and seductive. "My grandmother used to make me hot chocolate with chili every time I would get upset. It would always make me feel better."

"Seriously? I was just kind of improvising. I have never even heard of chili pepper in hot chocolate before." Joe smiles widely. "Did it work today? Do you feel any better?"

"You know what, I think it did. All things considered." She stops and looks around. "At least it may help me get through today."

"That is the best way to handle this place. If you start thinking about forever you will go mad. Just concentrate on today."

"Thank you," the pretty girl says as she stands and goes to the door. "Concentrate on today." She tells herself as she opens it and walks out into the orange haze.

Joe smiles to himself, feeling pretty darn good for a change. He turns and finds himself face to face with Captain Stan. Stan raises one stubby finger to motion to Joe back in the kitchen.

"Am I in trouble?" Joe asks with some concern.

Captain looks at him sadly. "Trouble, no. But gone? Yeah." He hands over a pink slip.

Joe looks at it with shock. On the bottom of the pink slip it says:

Terminated for Providing Comfort.

Joe is absolutely livid. Yes, he's pissed that Stan could not see past one itty bitty kind act, but he's angrier at himself. *Am I going crazy?* He wonders as he walks briskly toward the agency. *This is the second job I have lost in as many weeks.* First there was Joe's debacle at the superstore that got him fired from the Gazette, and now a pretty girl sheds a few tears and he's jumping around a kitchen like Wolfgang Puck.

Now he's got the distinct pleasure of telling Deedy that he's lost the very first temp job the agency secured for him. For a brief moment he is kind of bummed that Louise is not around. She might be able to tell him the best way to couch the information.

When Joe walks into the office there is Gabby standing there talking to Louise. *Be careful what you wish for.* Thinks Joe. *Damn it.* Louise is probably reporting to Gabby that he had ditched her this morning. In fact, they do seem to be talking when he approaches and when he gets close they clam up.

"Am I interrupting something?" he says.

"No not at all, I was just leaving," Louise says quickly. "Missed you this morning," she starts, then pauses to look at him closer. "Did you have an okay day?"

"Not really," Joe answers sorely.

"Yeah, well. What do you expect? Remember where we are!" she says with a smile. Then just as she is walking away toward the elevator, Deedy's voice comes booming from down the hall.

"Mr. Watkins, I presume?"

Gabby looks at him and with her head motions him back to the office.

When Joe walks into Deedy's office, he seems almost jovial. "Joe, my boy! Have a seat!"

Joe sits down and rubs his palms on his pirate britches to try to make them dry. "I have something I need to tell you," he says nervously. "I was…fired."

"Finally," Deedy responds. "Tell me what happened." Deedy sits behind his desk and folds his hands. "Tell me about it."

Joe relays the story about the hot chocolate. And about the subsequent pink slip.

"Why do you think you felt the need to help that poor girl?" Deedy says, opening up a file and grabbing a pen.

Joe's mind opens and is flooded with memories. He begins, "It was not my life's dream to be a paparazzi. I used to have real dreams of writing real books. I was going to write the great American Novel. I used to imagine myself becoming the new Twain. Or at the very least, a halfway decent facsimile of the new King."

"Oh, Stephen King? Did you write scary stories? I've always loved scary stories!" Deedy is excited now.

"No, it wasn't the genre, it was the notability. Writers that just seem to be able to come up with the perfect stories that will ensure their immortality, not to mention the ability to sell a gazillion books."

"Right. Gotcha. Perhaps those writers were able to refrain from diversions?" Deedy says playfully. Then he makes his signature move. At least Joe has seen him do it several times since meeting him. He sits back and props his feet up on his desk.

"Sorry. Anyway, when I was trying to write I would go to this diner near my apartment. I was so young and so full of affectation that I actually thought writing in a diner made me seem more talented."

"And it didn't?" Deedy asks innocently.

Joe decides to let that go. "One day I was sitting there just staring at a blank piece of paper, amazed at how empty my brain had become. This woman came in and sat directly across from me. I didn't even look up at her. She just started talking to me like we were old friends. When I finally did look up at her, only to confirm that I had never laid eyes on her before, she had already told me that her parents preferred her younger sister, she had recently dropped out of college, the fact that she had loved and lost three dogs in her lifetime, and I was pretty sure she was about to tell me exactly when her menstrual cycle started when I finally interrupted her. I thought I was going to tell her to shut the fuck up and leave me alone, but when I opened my mouth it was to ask her name." Joe stops to revel in this newfound memory, and to put a quarter in Deedy's curse jar.

"And that was terrible?" Deedy asks.

"No, it was incredible," Joe responds. "Tara was her name. She became my girlfriend. We were together for six years. To this day, those were the best six years of my life."

"What happened?" Deedy is continuing to make notes in his file.

"Well, I stopped writing. I became complacent. Then the job at the paper came, and I was getting a paycheck. Of course, all confidence and sense of self-worth bottomed out. I started to grow distant, more sullen with each passing day. Until…"

"Until?" Deedy sits up and leans forward.

"Until her father died. It was sudden, unexpected. Tara was devastated. But of course the funeral was uncomfortable. She and her sister getting competitive. Her mom, grief-stricken lashing out at her daughters. At one point, I took Tara's hand and started to walk. I really didn't have any idea where we were going until I looked up and realized we had arrived. At the diner. At our diner. We went inside and sat in our booth, we ordered hot chocolates, and we talked. We told stories about her dad, laughing and crying for hours." Joe now wipes a slight wetness out of the corner of his eye.

"You provided comfort. With hot chocolate," Deedy says.

"I guess I did. Of course, it still didn't last. We broke up within the year."

94

"But you broke up because you had completed your journey together. It was time to go your separate ways. Still, a nice memory though, am I right?"

"Yes, the best. And over time I really did enjoy my job," Joe says, finally relaxing after the emotional storm of remembering Tara.

"Speaking of enjoying your job," Deedy says. "How do you think you'd feel about working outdoors?"

"As opposed to hanging out in a giant grease trap?" Joe responds. "Sounds pretty sweet."

"Good. Well then, tomorrow you start in construction," Deedy says with authority.

"Wait." Joe panics just a bit. "Building things? Important things? I mean, nothing too important, right? No one will have to live in anything I build." He is actually getting scared. "Cooking with no experience is one thing. Buildings are big. They can fall down and land on people."

Deedy laughs. "You will be just fine. Tomorrow, dear boy, we shall see exactly what you can build." And he pushes a post-it note across the desk.

CHAPTER ELEVEN

So this whole guardian angel thing is getting a little sucky. First of all, Joe is doing everything he can to avoid me. To include leaving early so he can ditch me and walk to work all by himself. How are you supposed be a guardian angel to a son of a bitch like that? Second, I have to deal with my own residual amount of jealousy over the fact that he kept his job longer than a day. Gabby gave me the whole "everyone has to take their own journey" line of crap, but I can't help but feel slightly bruised in the ego department. That leads to other thoughts, like I wonder if Deedy likes him more than he likes me. And yes, I get that Deedy is the creator of all and loves each of us, but that is abstract. Once you accept that God exists and is capable of unconditional love, you can think in abstract terms, but on a limited level. How many religions in the land of the living not only deliver the message that God is real, but also feel the need to say they are the only one that is getting everything right? Why else would a person knowing that they are going to Heaven feel the need to not only need to believe, but also hang onto the idea that someone else is going to Hell? Sibling rivalry, that's why. And I hate to admit it, but after a few dozen years of actually being able to hang out with Him? I too sometimes forget, and become very protective of my own relationship with him.

"Isn't pride one of the seven deadly sins?" That smooth baritone fills my ears like chlorinated water in a swimming pool and sent a chill down my spine. I know that voice. My mystery man is back.

"Oh fabulous. More fucking intrigue," I say, while I think is he another telepath?

"Are you surprised there is more than one of us?" He decides to give up a little of his mystery. I don't know whether to be glad of that or scared.

"A little. Why haven't I met you before now?" There are many angels in Heaven. Billions of billions of people and at least millions of millions of angels. Way more than I could ever meet in a thousand years. That is not the point. The fact of the matter is this one is pissing me off.

And here's why. He is way too handsome for the comfort level of any human female. He is really enjoying the whole mystery man persona, which gives him an arrogant air, and he knows way too much about me. Hence I am going to be as snarky as I can possibly muster. And as much as an archangel will allow, I suppose.

"How come every time we meet, Ms. Patterson, you are in the street like a stray cat?"

Okay, so that makes me laugh a little.

"Guardian angel duty," I answer. "And I prefer feral cat."

"Hmmm...if your reputation is to be believed, I would have thought you'd be further advanced in your duties. Is there some reason you have not achieved your full potential?" He speaks slowly, almost like he is already bored with this conversation.

"And if my albeit limited experience with angels is correct, then you already know I asked for this assignment," I said with the sheer exasperation of a person who is already tired of this conversation.

"Guilty as charged. What I don't know is why." Now, he perks up, with a little curiosity.

"And I don't know you at all. Not even your name. So let's call it even, okay?"

He laughs a deep rough laugh and extends his hand. "Call me Mr. Lugner."

I am surprised. He just revealed two pieces of personal information in less than five minutes. Maybe if I continue to act like I couldn't care less who he is, I'll get even more. "Nice to know what to call you, Mr. Lugner. Whenever you successfully stalk me on the streets of Hell." I take his hand and instead of shaking, he pauses, just kind of holding mine. The gesture is without malice or a sense of the lascivious. It just feels…nice.

I enjoy the warmth of his touch for a moment before I pull back. "However, now I must go play chaperone to a construction worker." I turn to walk away from him.

"So soon? What a shame. We were just getting to know one another, Ms. Patterson. I do look forward to our next encounter."

"Yeah, well. You don't seem to have a problem finding me. It seems I don't have a choice as to whether or not there will be one. So, I will just say until next time," I say, sounding so much like the bitch I used to be, back in my breathing days. I almost get a little nostalgic for my former life.

Lugner turns and walks the exact same direction as I am heading. I don't want to look like I'm walking with him. I also don't want to look like I am following him. Damn, I thought these stupid social conundrums died when I did. Now, I walk in the opposite direction so that I can go around the block and end up coming from the other direction to Joe's construction site.

Even though I don't feel the heat the same way that the damned feel it, it is much warmer than it normally would be. It must be residual or something. So while for a Hell resident it feels like standing about six feet away from a bonfire the size of the State of Delaware, to me it feels like a normal summer afternoon in Vegas. Hot, but not Hell hot. Anyway, by the time I get to Joe, I am a sweaty mess.

Joe is walking off the site just as I approach. I immediately forget the hot mess I have become. Instead, I stand in the middle of the street, laughing out loud at poor Joe. He looks like a mental patient trapped in a sauna.

"Damn." Is all I can manage.

"Fuck you." Is all he can manage. Now we are both laughing.

As I walk and he hobbles toward the agency, I am thinking that I am making small talk, but in reality I am ranting about Lugner. Who does that guy think he is? Trying to be mysterious and incredible looking and throwing me off my game. Joe is listening, sort of.

"I'm not helping you at all, am I?" I say, realizing I've spent the last fifteen minutes on a giant Lugner diatribe.

"Well, the pain developing in my head is a distraction from the pain in my back. That counts as help," he says, laughing. "By the way, Louise, I am sorry about leaving early to miss you yesterday."

"So you admit it was to avoid walking with me?" I say.

"Yes. But not because I don't like you, and I actually missed talking to you. I just thought that maybe I needed some time to myself. Oh, and I know that you are a spy."

"A spy? Wow. I suddenly feel like a Bond girl!" I say with a flourish.

"You know what I mean. I know that you don't want to hang out with me, it's your job. I get that you are not really an elevator repair person." He smiles at me.

"You really are a tremendous guy Joe," I say warmly. "And by the way, I did do something to that elevator that day. I just haven't figured out if I was the one who fixed it, or if I was the one who broke it."

I leave him at the elevator doors this time, and give him a pat on the back as he goes inside.

"Not coming up?" he asks.

"No, I need to go see a friend," I say. What I can't tell Joe is that I can't face the emptiness of that place for me. So I just smile and say, "Good luck up there." And walk away.

But you know what? I wasn't lying about the friend. I am going to go hang out with Hank. I will tell him about my new job, and I will tell him why. We will talk about Joe and we will laugh about Lugner, and I will forget, at least for a brief moment that I am all alone again in Hell.

When I get to Hank's apartment, it begins to remind me of the old days when Linda and I were together day in and day out. He answers the door and greets me with a giant grin.

"Lou, if you are gonna keep hanging out here, then the refrigerator is over there." Hank knows from previous experience that I have no problem whatsoever in the "helping myself" department. If anything, he should be scared that I just may decide to make myself a four course meal while I'm in his kitchen. Of course, he also knows I don't cook. So instead I just go through the cupboards scrounging for chips and dip. I also fix myself and Hank sodas and bring everything out on a tray.

"Wow. Way to make yourself at home," he says, reaching for the chips.

"Sorry. I thought that was what you meant by pointing out the kitchen."

"It was. That's why I congratulated you," he says, laughing.

We settle back and start to talk about my new assignment. When I tell Hank that I am back in Hell acting as a guardian, of course he questions whether or not I have seen Linda. I explain to him that I probably won't see her, and that she can't see me. When he questions me further I have to tell him that right now I am blinded to a lot of things too. Particularly Deedy. And how that has been bothering me so much.

He comes over and sits on the side of my chair, putting his arm around me. "Louise, this is an amazing sacrifice you are making just for the chance that you may see Linda. You have no idea how grateful I am."

Then we start to talk about Lugner. Of course Hank is laughing as I convey the story of Lugner's appearances and his general mystery. However, after about a half hour he drops the big question.

"So why you?"

"I've been asking myself that too. I'm thinking maybe Deedy sent him?"

"Maybe, or perhaps you've become something to see, Lou. You know, asking for a demotion, agreeing to return to Hell, and I have heard that you have been having a constant argument with Deedy about not having wings?" he says with laughter.

"Hey! Like you don't secretly want them too. Who wouldn't want wings? And powers? The powers are the coolest part. Gabby and Lugner with their mind reading, and Gabby can heal. Who knows what else Lugner can do?"

"Louise, you know that those wings and powers come with a whole host of other obligations, right?"

"Well, yes. But think about that too. I mean, when was the last time you heard about a town getting smote, or some sighting of a host of angels in the sky? There's not too much field work left for an angel. Gabby makes coffee and ensures people get to their appointments on time. She's basically a coffee pot and alarm clock with the ability to rain fire down on a village if commanded to," I say.

"And which part of that do you aspire to be?" Hank asks.

"All of it, as long as it comes with a big set of pretty wings!" We laugh together, and continue for a while longer. When I leave I go back to my apartment and lie there, looking into the darkness. I say into it, even though I know that she can't hear, "Linda, know that you are loved." Then I drift off to sleep with a smile for the first time since taking this assignment.

CHAPTER TWELVE

Linda opens her eyes and slams her hand down on the alarm clock. She hates that thing with the same intensity she used to hate the cabbage soup diet that Louise used to make her go on with her all time. That stupid diet never made her lose two dress sizes as promised. It just gave her terrible gas and made her breath smell like a moose.

She doesn't even understand why they let you sleep down here. By the time she is able to think straight, she realizes she feels even more tired than she did when she went to bed. Is that more of Hell's magic? That sleep actually has the reverse effect on the body than it should?

She gets out of bed and makes her way around the room, avoiding the closet. She hates the closet most, and would rather take a beating than get dressed for her stupid job.

It's just all so pointless. Her job doesn't even make sense. She has met two of the three partners, both of whom are trolls sitting in dark offices all day doing fuck-all. They never see clients and they never leave to go anywhere like court, or to a bar, or anywhere else lawyers go to in Linda's imagination. However, they seem to produce an extraordinary amount of files. Which they then give to Linda so that she can run around and haphazardly place them in random drawers. Linda sighs heavily. *Give up trying to understand and just go.* She opens the door to the wretched closet. Today's torture du jour is a velour running suit the color of bubble gum. Why do they make clothes in neon pink? Is there anyone ever born who looks good in neon anything, let alone pink?

Is everything down here going to cause these futile

questions? Will she someday actually be used to her new life? Linda honesty doesn't think that will make her feel any better. She thinks that once you get used to being in Hell is when your soul is really damned.

She pulls on the tracksuit, puts her hair up in a messy bun, and heads down to the front desk. Rude Randy, who brought along a horrible case of adult acne, as well as a bad attitude, is still down engrossed in the computer. Linda has seen what is available on the computers down here, so she can only assume that Rude Randy has serious behavior disorders.

"Concierge," she says, her voice dripping in sarcasm." "Any messages for me?"

He doesn't even look up. He just reaches under the counter as though he's about to pull out a package or an envelope. He then pulls out his empty hand and presents Linda with a single finger.

Ha! Linda laughs as she walks out. Torturing rude Randy is the only fun she has down here. But with that done for the day, there is nothing left to do but go to her ridiculous job.

She stops for coffee, although, again she really doesn't understand why. The coffee shop on her way to work serves coffee that could be drunk with a fork. It tastes like old mud that some tribe of aboriginal people walked barefoot through on a regular basis. And this is not a tribe that subscribes to daily bathing. In short, the coffee sucks ass. But it's like a compulsion. Linda cannot seem to walk to work without stopping and getting a huge steaming cup of it.

She arrives at the office exactly twenty minutes late, which makes her the first one to arrive. She has to wait outside due to the fact that Suzy, the office manager who hired her, refuses to give her a key. Suzy actually refuses Linda everything. Ever since they had that little spat in front of Mr. Davis, she has made it her number one priority to make Linda's life even more miserable.

She even refused to tell Linda her name. And although Linda finally just labeled her with the moniker Miss Meany, and she was actually starting to answer to it, it did bother Linda more that she likes it admit. Finally one day, Linda learned her name by accident. She had to wait until one of the partners poked his head out and screamed Suzy's name.

So now Suzy likes to make sure Linda has no key, and Linda has to stand outside like a beggar until someone else shows up to let her in. While she waits, her attention is drawn to the construction site across the street. One guy in particular looks especially miserable. He's kind of stocky and sweating like a whore in church. Of course the suit complete with dress shoes are not helping matters. His closet is cruel. She looks down and once again is assaulted by the color and material of her own outfit.

Touché.

Mr. Morgan is the first to arrive. Right behind him is someone Linda doesn't know. Once they get inside, Linda discovers that the stranger is a potential client. An actual client! Linda is a little excited. Mr. Morgan just grumbles and goes to his office.

Linda follows him. "What should I do with the client?" she asks excitedly.

"Talk to him, find out why the hell he's here, tell him that we will call him if he has a case, then file your notes and forget you ever met him. What did you think you were supposed to do?" Mr. Morgan was always short on words and big on attitude.

"Got it." She turns and returns to the guy. "Please take a seat. Can I offer you something? Oh, wait, we really don't have anything." She realizes.

"That's fine. Can you just help me?"

Wow, this guy seems desperate. Linda thinks. Wonder if he has committed a horrible crime and wants us to get him off? Then she wonders, what could be considered a horrible crime down here? Smuggling in some really cute puppies? She laughs at the thought.

"Did I say something funny?" he says.

"No, I'm sorry. What were we doing?"

"You are going to help me?" He now looks a little frightened.

"Good. Okay." She opens up a Manila folder and grabs a notepad. "Let's start with your name." She holds her pen and tries to look official.

"Monroe Tice."

"And why are you here, Mr. Tice?"

"To get a divorce."

"A what?" Linda looks confused.

"A divorce? You know from my wife." Mr. Tice seems exasperated.

"Hold on," Linda says. Now she really is confused. With no other option, she approaches Mr.Morgan's door and nervously knocks.

"Mr. Morgan?"

"Is he gone?" he responds.

"Not exactly. He wants a divorce. Is that even possible down here?"

"Figure it out. Stop bothering me." Was the only response.

Okay, figure it out. Can you get a divorce in the afterlife? What happens? Once it's finalized they automatically reappear at opposite ends of the city to ensure that they never see each other? Suddenly there is a flash of inspiration. She rushes back to the desk and Mr. Tice.

"When you got married, Mr. Tice, it was until death

do you part. So now you're both dead, I'm assuming. Right?"

"Yes. But—"

"So your marriage is no longer valid!" Linda says excitedly. "Case closed. Thank you for your business." Linda shuts the manila folder.

"But no," Mr. Tice says.

"No what?" Linda reopens the folder.

"My wife, Charlotte, couldn't do anything like other people. Everything had to be an event like no other. We had a costumed wedding with people in masks, and she had some old pagan ceremony that instead of saying till death do you part it said in life and beyond. So technically we are still married. And stuck here together, and I swear if I have to live with her another minute I'm going to go mad. I mean, eternal damnation I get, and yes, our love of masks continued after our wedding...especially when we were robbing banks, which is what we did for a living until we were both shot in a standoff with the local police. So obviously we both deserve to be here...but come on! Can I get a break and at least suffer eternity alone like everyone else?"

Linda is shocked. Why would someone choose to be alone for eternity? Even if the person you are forced to be with is barely palatable. Linda would love to have someone to talk to or even scream at as opposed to being lonely all the time. She has murdered her husband and still she misses him every day.

"Mr. Tice. Are you sure? This may just be a lull in a very long, obviously fulfilling relationship," she starts.

"No! I am absolutely sure. You find a way to get her the fuck out of my life!" Mr. Tice is now angry.

This poor man in front of her has no idea what he is wishing for. Fortunately, her response is prepared.

"Well, we've got all the necessary information and

one of our partners will be in contact as soon as they have has a chance to review your case. Thank you for coming in." She stands and leads him to the door.

Thinking of Hank now makes her shift in her shoes and blink back tears. Everyone she loves is probably in Heaven all together. Happy and celebrating lives well lived. She alone must face the consequences of her wretched life.

After he's gone she turns and comes face to face with Suzy. She seems a bit shocked as Linda takes the Manila folder and files it away.

Linda tries to be casual. "You weren't here. Someone had to lose that guy. And did you hear why he was here? He wanted a divorce..." but she realized she was talking to herself. Suzy had turned and was chatting to herself, or so it would seem. Either that or an invisible client had just walked in. Suzy can really be very immature. She just can't stand anyone else having any responsibility. If she had her way…Linda feels a bit lightheaded. All of the sudden she feels like she is going to faint. Her peripheral vision starts to close in and there is a ringing in her ears. She grabs a desk to steady herself and hears her own voice speaking as if from far away.

"I think I need to get some air."

Suzy turns and looks at her with disdain. "Just go home," she says sharply.

So Linda goes home.

CHAPTER THIRTEEN

Poor Joe. He looks like reheated shit these days. Construction work is not agreeing with him. On the other hand, I do think he might be warming up to me. At least he hasn't tried to ditch me for a day or two. We have also managed to get past the small talk and we are well into the playful banter stage of our relationship. Of course, most of the playful banter is at my expense, but why should he be any different than anyone else, right? Nonetheless, I feel like he is much more comfortable with me since we had that little heart to heart. I'm still keeping a lot of information close to the vest, and he, with his mad reporter skills, knows this. Most of it is regarding Deedy. But it is easy for me to do, because I know what is in store for him.

Today we walk to the construction site in a comfortable silence. I certainly know why I don't feel like talking, but I am wondering why he's so introspective this morning.

"Penny for your thoughts," I say.

But Joe just gives me a sad smile. "Not even worth that much," he responds. Then he says, "Can I ask you a question?"

"Sure," I say with caution. Of course he can ask me any question. I'm just not sure that I am willing to answer every single one.

"What exactly do you do all day, while I'm at work?"

I look at him with a wide smile. "I'm off repairing elevators and stuff."

"And I am supposed to believe that even if that were true, there would be that many broken elevators? Or that even if they were broken, that the owners would want them to be fixed?"

I just laugh. "I never said it was a difficult job."

"Really, Louise, I wanted to talk about…you know."

"Do I?"

"Yes, Deedy. I know you work for him."

I have yet to confirm or deny that, and I am not about to now. "Do you wish I wasn't here, Joe?"

"No. I'm getting used to you." Joe smiles at me again.

"Then stop questioning why I am here," I say, casually brushing this line of questioning aside. "And instead tell me about construction."

"I'd rather not." He laughs. "Can you at least tell me something you have planned for the day? It might give me something to think about other than the fact that I'm sweating like a beer can at a summer picnic already."

"That tie can't help matters any. I get the whole suit thing, and the dress shoes really are a nice touch. But why did you wear the jacket and tie?"

"Everything is connected. There is no way to take part of it off. It looks like a three piece suit, but in reality it is a one piece suit." Joe just looks helpless.

"It really is kinda brilliant, in a completely sadistic way," I say, touching the fabric.

"So? What's on your schedule for today?" he says.

"Today I'm searching for someone. Lugner. I want to try to figure out what he's up to."

"Hey, I meant to ask you. Is he an attorney?" he asks.

"I don't know," I answer, looking at him hopefully.

"Well, my construction site is across from a law office. And Lugner is one of the names on the shingle. Davis, Morgan, and Lugner. Now, there could be a ton of Lugners down here, obviously. But it seems like a good place to start," Joe says.

"Cool! I start there first." This is exciting. I am bound

to find him before he finds me again. If he wants to play mind games, then he's met his match. No one plays mind games better than a woman who managed to stay jobless for the entire forty-five years she was alive.

Joe's interrogation brings up the lingering question in my own mind too. What if Lugner does work for Deedy and is supposed to be keeping an eye out for me? A compelling thought that makes me want to find Lugner even more than before.

After dropping Joe off at his site I first go in search of coffee. Yes, I am spoiled by my Heaven zip code and cannot imagine drinking a cup of coffee from my old stomping grounds, but I really need a caffeine boost. I stop by a small coffee shop and order a cup of their house blend. Their house blend is a cross between used motor oil and melted eyeliner pencil. I manage to choke most of it down as I sit and let Hell walk by me for a while. I figure a law office won't be hopping until mid-morning.

Once I am done, I go back to Joe's site, cross the street and find myself standing in front of a law office. I look at the sign and close my eyes. Can it really be this easy? Please let it be this easy. I stare at the name on the shingle. An archangel posing as an attorney in Hell? Guess it's no different that posing as a receptionist. Or God himself owning a temp agency.

I swing open the door and come face to face with a foul looking woman who turns from her desk to glare at me.

"Hi. I'm looking for Mr...." I say, avoiding her glare.

She registers surprise. "Do you have an appointment?"

"No. We met recently, and I just wanted to follow up with him. Is he here?" Why won't she just tell me if he's around? Damn, I hate gate keepers.

She steps closer to me and looks me up and down.

"Are you here to sign a contract?"

What kind of contract would I possibly be signing after just meeting him? "No, we have not discussed any particulars," I say, giving away no information but still relaying a sense of urgency.

"Oh. Well then, I must be confusing you with someone else," she says, still not smiling.

"Can I see him?" I am pretty sure I've asked that several times.

"No, he is not here." And that's that. Now she's done with me.

But I'm not done with her. "Are you expecting him back today? Would it be better for me to wait or to make an appointment to come back?" That's my polite way of saying I'm not going anywhere, bitch.

"Not if he's not expecting you. He's not here. He's almost never here." Then she turns away from me and looks to her side as if she cannot stand to look at me any longer. And then she says, quite rudely, "Just go home!"

"Fine! You don't have to get shitty about it," I say, then I turn to leave.

Suddenly out of the corner of my eye I see a pink flash, and get overwhelmed by a familiar feeling. Out of my peripheral vision I see her. Linda is here! When I turn to see her, she disappears. I run outside. Did she come out here? I look up and down the street but there is no trace. Did I just imagine her? I don't think so. This feeling is so strong, unlike anything I've ever experienced before. And if I were going to imagine Linda, I highly doubt that I would imagine her in a pink track suit. Obviously she was dressed by her Hell closet! This was real. She was here.

But now she is nowhere to be seen. I even shout out her name outside, but of course there is no answer. I sink down on the curb and feel the tears start. I am so grateful to have seen her, but I also feel my soul ache that she is here.

I stand up with a renewed sense of purpose. Who cares about a mystery angel? I really don't care right at this moment if Joe feels warm fuzzy thoughts about me either. All I can think or care about right now is Linda. Finding her again, reaching her. I start almost running down a side street, searching for a sign of pink. When I do not see her I go faster, not slower. Then I turn another corner and run smack dab into...

Lugner.

Are you fucking kidding me? "Whoa!" I say as I look up and recognize him immediately. "Watch where you're going, Lugner!"

"I apologize, but what a happy accident this is." He seems genuinely shocked that I'm in front of him.

"Accident? So, you don't know that I was just in your office? By the way, kudos on the customer service. That woman you have in the front is not ever going to make it onto anyone's Christmas card list."

"Ah. That would be Suzy. You were in my office?" he asks curiously.

"Yes, I figured I would just appear like you usually do so you'd have an idea of how incredibly creepy that actually is," I say. "But I guess it didn't work, because all I got was the pleasure of Suzy, and you still managed to scare the pants off of me."

"I am sorry. For both scaring you and subjecting you to Suzy. I must say I'm a bit impressed. No one ever comes looking for me. That is why I have such refined stalking skills," he says teasingly.

"It's not funny. The last thing I needed today was another scare," I say, holding onto my chest, feeling my imaginary heart beat out a rumba rhythm.

"Seeing Linda scared you? I would have thought you would have gotten some pleasure out of that experience," he says casually.

"How…what…were you?" I can't even finish a thought. My head is spinning now. How could he have possibly known? It wasn't like I was thinking about Linda or anything.

"Well, Louise, I obviously know who is in my employ. And if you were in my office, then obviously you saw her," he says.

"But I wasn't sure that I had." "Yes, Deedy's magic is still holding. For now," he says, mischievously.

"Do you think she saw me?" I ask hopefully.

"No, I'd say she probably felt a little dizzy and went home early," he concluded. "However, I think I can be of assistance to you, Louise, if you like."

"Help me do what?" I say.

"Help you do what you came to do. Come to my office in the morning. I can explain everything to you."

"Okay. Tomorrow, after I drop Joe off," I say, and we wave and go our separate ways.

I could actually be seeing Linda as soon as tomorrow! But instead of feeling elated, I start to feel uneasy. What does he mean he can help? And what was the stuff about Deedy's magic? Why do I find Lugner both thrilling and disturbing? Ugh.

I just don't feel much like talking anymore tonight. And with seeing Linda for just a split second, I'm not sure about seeing Hank. So I decide to skip any visiting and go straight back to my apartment. Tomorrow is a new day. And it may be one of the most important days I have had here so far.

CHAPTER FOURTEEN

Joe is working hard, sweating terribly, and hates this stupid suit. John, the foreman on this construction site also demands that he wear a tool belt. The suit looks even more ridiculous with his tool belt strapped over it. He is missing a ton of tools, just one more reason he hates the belt. So he is forced to run around and beg or borrow tools all the time.

He has been stuck working outdoors since he started. Today, he starts outside and right after lunch he is sent inside. He is glad for the change of scenery. Until he sees what kind of scene it really is in there.

Joe finds himself working with Abe and Charlie. Abe is a very large, very mean man who pretty much keeps to himself. Charlie is more like a prison guard. Not exactly friendly, but seems a little more fair. At one point John comes in and hands Joe a shelf.

"Put this up over the toilet in the bathroom," he barks at Joe.

"I'll need a hammer and a level," Joe says, looking down at his useless tool belt.

"Why would you need a level?" John seems confused.

"Right. Sorry, I must have been delirious for a minute. But a hammer? That seems pretty necessary." Joe realizes there is no need to make a shelf level because that would make it functional. Joe cannot even recall a single shelf in his apartment, let alone one that you could actually set things on.

"Borrow a hammer from Abe or Charlie," John says.

Joe sighs and goes back inside, trying to steel himself to ask either one of those two for a favor. However, once he gets into the kitchen area he sees a hammer sitting on the table. He just picks it up and carries it to the bathroom where he starts on the shelf. After about an hour, it is all done. He stands back to admire his handiwork when he hears shouting downstairs. The guys must be arguing again, for the hundredth time this week. But when he hears a crash and glass breaking, he runs back through the house to where the boys are now engaged in what seems to be a fistfight.

"I gave it to you! Give it back!" Charlie yells at Abe.

"I don't have it! You must have taken it back!" Abe is towering over Charlie, but that doesn't stop Charlie from still lunging at Abe. Abe picks up a stray board off the floor and plants it hard on the side of Charlie's head. Charlie returns the favor by grabbing a chair and breaking it over Abe's head.

"What the fuck is happening here!" John says as he rushes in and stands between the two of them.

"Charlie has lost his ever loving mind!" Abe says.

"He's a thief, and he's got my hammer!" Charlie growls

"A hammer? All of this is over a hammer?" John asks. "You two would kill each other, if that were possible, over a damn hammer? I should can both of you, right here. Let me make this very clear. Are you both listening?" He waits for Abe and Charlie both to confirm. "When I find that hammer I may just use it to brain you both. But I will definitely fire whoever has it. Comprende?"

"Nice knowing you," Abe says to Charlie.

"Have fun asking for change in front of the diner," Charlie responds.

"That won't be necessary," Joe says.

John turns around and sees Joe approaching. "This isn't about you, Joe. Go back to work."

Joe reaches into his tool belt and takes out the hammer. "I found it. Sitting on the kitchen table. I used it to hang that shelf. It was me. Please don't brain these two, and I will be waiting out in your trailer for my pink slip." He sets the hammer on a side table, smiles at Abe and Charlie, then walks out.

Out in John's foreman's trailer, Joe sits calmly while John is slamming things around like a child having a tantrum. Joe doesn't seem to understand the issue.

"What exactly is the problem? You said, whoever has the hammer goes," Joe says.

"Yeah, but I didn't mean it. I mean, really. If we fired everyone who stole something at a construction site there wouldn't be anyone left," John says.

"Okay. So again, what is the problem? Just yell at me and send me back on the job."

"Yeah, can't do that either." John seems torn.

"Why?" Joe is partly confused, partly just tired of this and wants it to end.

"Joe, I think I still have to fire you. But not because you took the hammer. Because you gave it back." John looks at him with sad eyes. "Here ya go, Joe. Sorry." And hands Joe his slip.

Terminated for Trustworthiness.

Joe is actually fine. It seems like this is supposed to be what happens with temp jobs from Deedy. You lose them, you go tell Deedy, and everything is honky dory. The only disconcerting thing about losing a job is that it unlocks another memory of his life. Joe is very comforted by the fact that his memory is like Swiss cheese from his days of being alive. Getting all these new flashes from the past is not the comfort that Deedy may think it is. It actually makes him kind of angry sometimes. Because most of those memories show Joe that his life overall was pretty decent.

At Deedy's office Gabby is waiting with ice cold root beer and a smile. Deedy looks at his pink slip and is almost celebratory about it.

"Terminated for Trustworthiness. Can't wait to hear about that. Come in, please." Joe sits in his usual chair across from Deedy's desk and tells him all about the war that was waged over a stupid hammer.

"Abe and Charlie seem like the kind of guys who like to use their fists to blow off steam," Deedy says finally. "You probably did them a favor, giving them a reason to beat the stuffing out of each other."

"I guess. Good thing John didn't think the same thing. Otherwise the pink slip would have said I was fired for trustworthiness and providing stress relief for my co-workers," Joe says.

Deedy laughs. "Let's talk about your stress level. How do you feel?"

"Okay. Why don't you ask what you really want to know?"

Deedy looks bemused. "What do I really want to know?"

"Memory," Joe says. "And yes, I have one."

Deedy says nothing. Just sits back and assumes his listening position. Joe begins.

"In the early 70s I met a young assistant to a very famous actress. She was a good girl, from a small town in the Midwest who came to the big city with a suitcase and a dream. You know, it's an old, old story. She wanted to be an actress, but ended up having to work for one. And man, she picked the worse one. This diva was horrible to her. She used to do things like try on twelve different outfits, make Sarah take photos of her in all of them, then make her go to a one hour film developer, get them developed and bring them back so she could pick the most photogenic outfit. She was abusive and exploited Sarah like she was an indentured servant. She would demand the most unreasonable things at the most unreasonable times, and Sarah always delivered. When I met her, I offered her some real money for any of those photos that were very unflattering. She refused. The actress was arrested for a DUI and threw her purse at Sarah when she came to pick her up from jail. I offered her money again for an inside scoop of her condition that night. She refused, again."

"Sounds like a lovely girl," Deedy says.

"Yes, she was. She eventually got fired after the actress publicly accused her of leaking a story about her going into rehab. I knew it was bullshit, because I knew Sarah would never have done that. I went to Sarah and told her as much. I also gave her a contact of a theater producer that I knew. He gave her a small part in his upcoming play. I went on opening night and was so pleased for her. Even though it was a small part, she had made it her own and stole the show. She got more parts, bigger parts, and eventually made the jump over to film. She became somewhat famous. Not Meryl Streep kind of famous, but she worked steadily and won a few awards. The thing is, once the papps were interested in her, she called me. She gave me every single scoop about her and supplied me with photos and everything. We became friends over the years. She made me a better reporter, because I stopped offering assistants to hand over unflattering photos and sneaking around alleys or digging through trashcans. I started developing real relationships with sources. Prove to them that you are trustworthy and they will be just as good to you. That became my motto."

"Good motto," Deedy says.

"Oh, and the actress that fired Sarah? Turns out she had planted that story herself. Her career was lagging, and she couldn't get work, so she decided an interesting tidbit in the tabloids would spurn interest in her again. The reporter she met with retired and wrote his memoirs. In them he admitted she had given him the story. It was fabulous. Talk about getting press interest? She got so much bad publicity that no one in Hollywood would touch her ever again." Joe laughs.

"So by choosing to be trustworthy instead of dealing in low grade gossip, didn't that mean that you were regularly scooped?" Deedy asks.

"Sure. That's why I never made it to the big time. But it also meant that I never got named in lawsuits or had to retract anything I'd put in print. And sometimes I would get a story that no one else would because celebrities that value their privacy would entrust me with the few secrets that they were willing to let out," Joe says, suddenly feeling sad. He thinks he may start to cry, and that fact is both shocking and horrible to him.

"My boy," Deedy says in his grandfatherly way. "What you need is just a tiny push and it may be sooner rather than later that you start to fly!" Deedy was always saying weird things like that.

"Push me where?" Joe asks. "Or more importantly, push me off of what?"

Deedy laughs out loud at that. "Nothing too scary, Joe. I'm sending you back to the scene of the crime, as they say in the movies." He slides a yellow post-it note across the desk.

Joe picks it up and it is his turn to laugh. "Are you serious?"

"Go on. You might find it a more rewarding job than you think," Deedy says, looking at Joe kindly.

"As a cashier at a superstore? I can't imagine what could be rewarding about that," Joe says. "But what the heck, I'll give it a try."

"Tremendous!" Deedy exclaims. Sometimes his enthusiasm is a bit over the top.

As Joe walks home, he is lost in thought. Deedy has been good to him, and he feels better than he has felt since dying. Gabby and Louise are also part of it, providing him with more comfort than he has ever known in Hell. He just wonders, with this wild ride he's on whereby he gets a job, loses it, goes and gets another one. Exactly where does this ride go?

CHAPTER FIFTEEN

Linda wakes up from the weirdest night ever. Dreaming, in Hell. Go figure? Linda's night was filled with dreams. She isn't sure whether she should feel comforted or terrified by the images that haunted her overnight.

She was young again and happy and with Louise her best friend. They were walking down the street of some strange city in which Linda was pretty sure she had never been, and they were walking and laughing. Suddenly Louise looked at her with a strange expression and said, "I don't think I'm supposed to be here." And she turned around and left.

Linda stopped her and said, "You aren't just going to leave me here, are you? Isn't there something you can do?"

Louise gave her a lovely smile and said, "It doesn't work that way. Sorry, babe. See you on the flipside!" She winked as Lou used to always wink, then disappeared.

All of a sudden Linda was at her office complete with the dour attorneys and witchy Suzy. She said, "I'm looking for my friend." Absolutely no one was paying attention to her, so she started searching the office. She was looking through cupboards and drawers as if she was going to find Louise crouched inside of one of them. Then she saw her walk out the door. She ran after her screaming her name. "Louise, don't leave me here! Louise!"

Then Louise was gone.

Linda wakes up with tears streaming down her face. She feels abandoned by a ghost.

When Linda met Louise for the first time, it was

almost comical. Linda was in the throes of her own personal rebellion, against a solid middle-class suburban upbringing. Mostly she was just bored.

Her mom and dad wore down their knees and ran their throats dry with prayers for Linda. The funny thing is they were probably praying for a new influence on their daughter, who they felt was naïve and impressionable. But what they didn't realize was Linda always made her own choices. Including the fact that she was already pulling back from the scene and from the friends that made her parents nervous. She would just hang out every once in a while, and one of those nights Louise walked in. Boom…the answer to her parents' prayers. A brand new influence named Louise Patterson.

The mutual attraction between Linda and Louise was instant and intense. Linda never understood why Lou was so insistent that they become best friends, but she was grateful for it. She jumped on the bestie bandwagon immediately and the two of them became inseparable.

Louise was not just bigger than life, she was enormous. Exciting and adventurous, she always had a plan. Even if that plan was to do absolutely nothing for days. In fact, that was Louise's signature move. Doing fuck-all for days and days and days, and still having more fun and more laughs than anyone else.

Linda loved Louise like a sister, and at some point the friendship had transcended into something much more familial than anything she had known. When Louise named her daughter Linda, that was it. She became Aunt Linda and set out to spoil her name sake rotten.

After Louise died of breast cancer, Linda was devastated. It felt like someone had pulled a plug inside of her and let her soul drain away. She became obsessed with "Dinny"—little Linda's nickname—and became a second mother for her. Dinny was so small when Louise had passed, but she had her mother's pluck as well as her eyes. The two Lindas helped each other heal.

The point of this is Linda and Louise had always saved each other. Yet, in her dream Louise had walked away. What was her subconscious telling her? That she doesn't need saving. She is not convinced of that. That Louise is saving her, but not the way she wants? She would like to believe that is true. She wonders if Louise is happy, and secretly hopes that she is.

Linda still feels discombobulated and weird as she gets to work. She immediately picks up a stack of folders and starts to file them. She is still trying to shake off the previous night when all of a sudden Suzy looks at her with disdain.

"Do you think you are going to get overtime?"

"What?" Linda says.

"We don't pay overtime. It's time to go. Get the fuck out," Suzy says.

Linda is now very confused. "Are you high?" she says to Suzy. "What are you talking about? I've been here for like five minutes."

Suzy says, "Obviously I'm not the one with deficient mental capacity. You've been here all day."

Linda doesn't understand. "What?" She looks around and sees everyone else leaving. The partners are all getting their briefcases and walking out the door. Suddenly she feels tears behind her eyes. "Suzy, can I ask…what did I do all day?"

Suzy just rolls her eyes. "Not much. Threw some files around, as usual," she answers tersely.

Linda is astounded. How could she have lost all that time? Now she starts to panic. Maybe there is something else going on. Maybe there's an even greater punishment waiting for her around the corner.

Linda runs outside and sits down on the curb. She

starts to cry now. Heavy sobbing that makes her feel like she's choking out in this horrible heat. She closes her eyes and imagines being back in her room and decides she is just going to sit there on the curb hugging her knees for quite a long time.

* * *

I wake up feeling as excited as a kid on Christmas morning. This day feels important. When I meet Joe in the morning I am surprised, first by his hysterical outfit, and second when he tells me that he's starting a new job at the superstore today.

"Sorry about your luck, pal," I say through gales and gales of laughter.

"It can't be as bad as construction," Joe says, but still looks a bit miserable.

"Well, the good news is you'll be beating off all those painted women, they are gonna love you." I laugh some more at him. One of the trademarks of the girls who work in the superstores is that they get so bored, what with not helping customers that they just reapply their makeup over and over again. It would be funny if it wasn't so pathetic.

"Hey, there's something to look forward to." Joe's sarcasm is thick, and we are both laughing. "What's up with you?" he asks.

"Nothing much. Just hanging around," I say nonchalantly. I don't want to give away too much.

"Oh. Because Gabby said something kind of interesting," he says.

"What did she say?" Damn, she's been tuning in on me.

"She said today I'll be thinking of both of you, and hoping for the best." "Well, that's nice of her. I guess," I say, a little unsure.

When we get to the superstore, I give Joe a slap on the back and wish him good luck. As he walks away, I wolf whistle at him, then fall apart one more time over his clothing. Then I wait until he's safe inside before I leave to head to the law office. I know I'm going to arrive about the same time as the employees, and I feel so nervous. It's like I am about to meet a rock star or something, not reunite with my oldest and dearest friend.

When I arrive at the agency, Lugner is waiting for me outside. "Hello there, Louise. So glad you actually showed up."

"Of course I showed up. Was there any question?" I ask.

"With you humans, there is always a question. Free will and all that jazz." He chuckles. "Are you ready to go in?"

"Sure. Is there anything I need to know before I do?" I say with sudden concern.

"You will be able to see Linda, but not communicate with her. She won't know you are here. She will be totally unaware of her surroundings."

"That is better than nothing, I guess," I say with a bit of disappointment.

"Then let's go." He waves his arm across the door. A light emanates from his fingertips and covers the entrance. Then it seems to come to life all on its own and it swirls its way inside before us.

Now it is our turn. He opens the door and holds it for me, and we enter. The infamous Suzy looks up from her desk. First registering Lugner, then me. "Good morning, Mr. Lugner. How wonderful to see you here!" Sycophantic bitch.

"Good day, Suzy. This is my new friend, Louise. I understand the two of you met yesterday." His oozing charm has just a hint of underlying antipathy.

I smile and force myself to be polite. "Hello again."

She looks surprised. I guess Lugner doesn't bring folks around here very often. "Hello…yes…Ms. Patterson. So glad the two of you were able to catch up." Her discomfort gives me a small sense of pleasure. I look up at Lugner and grin.

"Louise, let's go into my office." He starts to guide me through the office. We do pause in front of a row of filing cabinets. I look up and catch my breath. My hand flies up to my mouth to stifle a scream as I look at one of the loveliest sights I've ever seen in Hell. My Linda!

She looks like a robot, or an automaton. She is just opening up cabinets and filing folders without even looking at them. Her face is expressionless and her movement unnatural.

"What is going on? Why is she like that?" I say to Lugner.

"In my office, Louise." He rushes me into his sanctuary and closes the door behind me. "I had to put a veil over her. She is not in pain, nor is she suffering. In fact, today will fly by for her. She will have no memory of being cloaked at all."

"But why? I thought the camouflage Deedy gave me would render me invisible to her anyway. Why does she have to be all…hypno-zombie?"

"That is an interesting point. The fact that you could see her yesterday, even just for a split second, and she felt your presence even if she couldn't actually visualize you, means that your connection is so deep that ordinary safety protocols do not fit. Pretty impressive, to be honest with you."

"So you could remove the veil, and we could talk."
"That would be a very bad idea, Louise."

"Why? Because it's against the rules?" I start to get

angry.

"Because it would be an exercise in torment for Linda," he says quietly.

"Oh." I sit down hard in a chair across from his desk.

"You can't just pop in and say hi, then go back to Heaven and leave her behind. For her, it would be unbearable. Imagine what would have happened if Bobby or Dinny had turned out to be real when you were here, and after they stopped by for a visit they went away and you were stuck at IP&FW."

I thought about that for a minute. Yes, that would have been beyond awful. The only comfort in remembering them and seeing visions of them was that once I remembered, I was brought into Heaven. So I decided to take the leap and say what was in my secret heart.

"So can't I bring her back with me?"

"That is what we have to discuss. Deedy has given you express instructions to not get involved. Now, obviously when and if Linda were to suddenly show up with you in Heaven, Deedy would welcome her with open arms. He's never going to deny anyone who was lost and is now found. That is just his way. But, he will intervene if he knows that you plan to extract her early."

"And he will probably be really mad at me," I say, getting a little pouty.

"I can't imagine he would be pleased," he says with a low laugh. "However, I can veil both of you and you can take her unseen into the pearly gates. Once you enter the WF&PI building the veil will disappear and Linda will be in Heaven." Lugner is now reaching into his desk to pull out some papers.

"So, what is in it for you?" I say to him.

"Do you ask Gabby what's in it for her every time she makes you coffee or brings you comfort?" He looks wounded.

"No, I guess not," I say apologetically.

"Okay then. Shall we go ahead and make a plan?" He looks at me expectantly.

"I need a minute. Can I answer you tomorrow?" I ask. I feel the need to step on the brakes a little.

Lugner looks a bit annoyed, but he answers me with a sweet, "Of course, I would not expect anything less from you, Louise."

I thank him profusely and walk out into the main office. I stop and just watch Linda for a little while. I discover that tears are flowing down my cheeks after a few minutes. "I love you, Linda," I say to the robotic woman moving around in front of me. She is oblivious. I then walk out the door and start to sob.

I knock on Hank's door, and when he answers, I leap into his arms. I'm crying so hard I can barely speak.

"Lou! What's wrong?" Hank is concerned, and he carries me inside. "Can I get you some water?" He runs to the kitchen and fixes me something to drink.

When I get myself together, I look at him with huge, wet eyes. "I need to talk to you." He sits across from me, and I tell him about Lugner, about my visit to his office today, about Linda and seeing her, and finally about Lugner's offer.

Hank leaps up from his chair and kneels before me. "So what is the question? Of course you are going to do it, right?"

"I don't know. I have to wrap my head around it," I say.

"Wrap your head around what? You could save her!"

"I'm just not sure that I am supposed to save her."

"Do you think you are supposed to leave your best friend in Hell?" He sounds a little angry. "Lou, you have to do it. Go home, think on it, get right with it. Whatever.

But in the end, just do it. For Linda and for me." Hank is pleading with me. I don't think I can take that anymore either, so I get up to go.

"Thanks, Hank, I will talk to you tomorrow." I make my way to the door.

"Okay, but Louise?" I turn and face him. "Ask yourself this question. Would Linda do it for you?"

Of course Linda would do it for me. Probably without question. Am I so terrible that I can't just run back to Lugner and say "Let's do it!" without hesitation? I just feel that something is not right. I can't shake it. So I go back to my apartment and get ready for bed.

I lie down in the emptiness of the night and let the dark fold over me. I realize I hate the dark now, like that awkward kid in high school, with its quietness and its need to invade your personal space. I jump up and turn on a small lamp on the other side of the room, giving just enough illumination to bully the protrusive dark away. I scurry back to my bed and pull the covers around my eyes to hide the light. I do this with as little sense of irony as I can possibly muster. I am drifting off to sleep when I decide to just go ahead and throw it out there. "Please help me? Send me a sign?" I mentally try to push the thoughts through my own veil and straight to Deedy's ears. I then send up the wish that I hope he gets the message. Finally true darkness overtakes me. And then I dream.

Linda and I are young again and walking together in a wooded area. Like hiking, which is funny because Linda and I never went hiking. We are walking and talking and laughing just like we used to do, and I feel so happy. Then we come to a fork in the path. One side is dark and filled with underbrush. It looks creepy, so I turn to the other path that is much more open. I say to Linda, "Let's go down here. It looks way better."

Linda looks at me and says, "That is your way. This is mine. We can't go together. This is where we have to part ways."

"But, Linda, I know the way down this path. Come with me." I sound desperate now.

"I can't. I have to go my own way." She sounds so calm, even as she's walking into the darkness.

I find myself crying now. "But, you'll get lost," I say to her, pleadingly.

"And I will find my way out," she says. "Don't worry. I will meet you on the other side. Just wait, be patient."

"Wouldn't you rather be able to see everything? You can if you will just follow me," I say, making one last ditch effort to keeping her safe.

"See everything? If I follow you, the only thing I will be able to see is your back. I really must go. If you love me, you will let me." And then she disappears into the darkness.

I wake up to the sound of my own sobs. I fall to my knees and don't even care if there is no one out there to hear me. "Thank you. Thank you for my sign. I now know what to do. Thank you."

Now all I have to do is hope I have the courage to do it.

CHAPTER SIXTEEN

Joe stands in front of his closet with his mouth open in a silent scream of horror. *They can't be serious.* He thinks as he takes out an old fashioned hospital gown. *Not only do I have to go to work as a cashier in a superstore, but I will also be mooning everyone in the process?* He digs around inside the closet, hoping against hope that there is underwear. Of course there is not. Maybe if he gets to work early, he will have time to purchase a pair before his shift. Then all he has to do is to also hope that they stay together long enough to make it through the day. The underwear sold in the superstore usually doesn't keep its elastic longer than juicy fruit gum keeps its flavor. In other words, ten minutes and they are around your ankles. Still, that is all he's got, so he gets dressed quickly. Not that it takes long to slip into a gown, and heads downstairs.

Louise has just arrived, and she can't stop laughing. She is in a state of delirious convulsions, and Joe thinks he may have to slap her to bring her back to being reasonable. Not that he would mind slapping her right about now.

After Louise pulls herself together, they walk to the superstore in pretty mild conversation. Of course she's enjoying his predicament a little too much, and he gets the sense that she may be hiding something about her own day's plans from him. But they get there, and she wishes him luck before he enters the store alone.

Inside, he heads straight for the underwear and pulls a pair off the shelf. Then he approaches one of the sales girls and asks for the manager. She rolls her eyes, but then she sees his outfit and stares openly at him for a full thirty seconds.

"The manager, now," he says to her sharply.

In about ten minutes the manager appears, and he introduces himself. The manager is an older man with about seven hairs still hanging on for dear life in his head. They are all white. He is short, about five feet two inches, and he is a bit...well, squirrely is the first word that comes to Joe's mind. Like he's always nervous. His small brown eyes are constantly darting back and forth like he's waiting for some employee to jump out and punch him. His name is Martin. He doesn't seem to notice the fact that Joe's ass is hanging out. He just launches into his spiel.

"Okay, here is where your register is going to be. In books and stationary. It is the least busy of all of our departments so it should be pretty easy. If anyone comes in and wants to know how to find a product, you just send them to Betty. She will be working at the register next to you, and she has been here for a while, so she knows the ropes. Other than directing customers to her, I would not talk to Betty. She doesn't have the best disposition." Betty looks up from her magazine to gaze over at Martin. He physically jumps at her stare. She then turns to Joe and looks him up and down, very slowly. It feels almost intimate, and Joe can feel color warming his face. Then he meets her eyes and she just starts to laugh.

"I'm happy to amuse," Joe says with a bow. Then he turns to Martin. "Can I pay for these before I start? I'd like to rectify my current situation."

Martin looks down and notices what Joe is wearing for the first time. "Oh my goodness. Don't worry! Just go put them on. Put something on." Then he scurries away.

Joe looks around for a restroom or a changing room, but doesn't see anything nearby. So he just goes behind his counter and slips on the underwear. Feeling a little better, he thinks he's ready for his day.

And man, is it a long damn day. When Martin said this was not a popular department he was being understated. It actually seems like the only customers who come into the books and stationary department are the ones who wander in by accident. Joe has only rung up two people in the last four hours. Betty is a bit of a freak show too. One customer came in looking for electronics, and she lunged at him with a steak knife. Another one asked them if they carry greeting cards, and Betty started throwing books at her. But not before she set fire to them. Yeah, throwing flaming books at customers. That is Martin's idea of a "not nice disposition." Joe laughs at his own thoughts.

Suddenly, there is a youthful looking man walking through the department. And he has a book in his hand. This could be an actual customer. Joe stands and looks expectantly at the boy. The young man walks up and puts the book on the counter.

"I would like to return this," he says.

Joe notices that Betty has stood up and is rolling up her sleeves. He catches her eye and says, "I'll take care of this one, Betty." She sits down, but continues to give the man the fish eye.

Joe looks at the book and notices that it's *A Tale of Two Cities*. "This has always been one of my favorites," he says to the young man. "Why would you want to return it?"

"You have read it before?" he asks Joe.

"Yes. Many times," Joe answers.

"Well, I haven't. This was my first time," the man says.

"And, you didn't like it?" Joe asks.

"Look at the end," the man says.

Joe flips through the book to the last page. It ends

with Sydney being led to the prison. Then it just stops. "It is missing the last page," Joe says incredulously.

"Which is why I need to return it."

Joe walks with him to the section of the books where Tale of Two Cities would be. He picks up another copy and goes to the end. The last page is also missing. There is one more copy. Joe picks it up, holding out little hope. He turns to the back and finds that the last page is missing. "They are all incomplete."

The young man looks dejected. "Now I will never know how it ends."

Joe says, "Come here." And sits the young man down on a stool by his register. "Stanly Carton goes to the prison where they are keeping Darnay. He convinces him to change clothes with him, then he drugs him so the guards will carry him away. Then Carton takes Darnay's place at the guillotine, where he is executed."

"Wow. That is kind of a stupid thing to do," the young man mumbles.

"Well, he does it so that he can give his life meaning. He says something really great at the very end," Joe replies.

"Do you remember it?"

"Yes, I think I do. He says 'It is a far, far better thing that I do, than I have ever done; it is a far, far better rest that I go to than I have ever known'."

"That's nice. Guess he didn't end up here, eh?" The boy laughs at his own joke.

"Guess not," Joe says. "You still want to return the book?"

"Nah. I'll keep it, if you don't mind writing that part about going to a better place in the back of it?"

"Sure. I certainly will." Joe writes the quote complete with crediting it to Charles Dickens and hands the book back to the young man.

He watches the man walk toward the exit and sees Martin coming at him at lightning speed. "Joe. I need to speak with you in the back."

Joe walks with him to the back and feels a stone forming in his belly. He knows this is not going to end well. He gets back there and there it is, on the table waiting for him. A pink slip.

Terminated for Fostering Closure

Joe grabs it and leaves. He storms out and starts walking toward Deedy's office. This is getting old fast. What is the point of having a job for four fucking hours? How is he going to explain this? Then he stops, in the middle of the street and grabs his head. Memories are rushing back to him now. He is suddenly laughing and crying at the same time. Oh, so many beautiful thoughts flowing through him. Why is he here? Why was he damned for all eternity? He must get to Deedy. He must explain.

He doesn't even feel like stopping for a chat with Gabby drinking root beer. He wants Deedy to know what he remembered. Gabby seems to sense that and sends him directly back to Deedy's office. He goes in and sits down.

"Fired again. But guess what I remembered?" Joe says excitedly.

"Tell me everything!" Deedy says.

"I didn't kill Tommy! He didn't kill himself because of me!" Joe says excitedly.

"Of course he didn't," Deedy says.

"No, I mean. Tom was sick. It was cancer of the stomach. He knew he was dying, and he wanted to clear everything up before his time. He came to me and asked me to out him. I wrote the story almost exactly like he told me. I even gave him a preview copy for his final approval. He was so glad, so grateful to me for putting it out there the way he wanted. So that his family would not have to deal with it after his death."

"And it seems that you did a wonderful job. That is why he felt okay leaving a little earlier than scheduled," Deedy says with so much caring.

"Speaking of that, he committed suicide."

"Yes, he did."

"Did he end up here?" Joe asks.

"No. He's happy now, and with his loved ones," Deedy responds.

"Good. That is good to hear." "Well, son. I think you are ready for a very big job." Deedy gives him a yellow post-it note.

Joe looks at the address. "I know this place. Louise was going there."

"Yes, that's the place," Deedy says, as if he knows all about Louise. "You start tomorrow." Deedy watches him with great concern in his eyes.

Joe feels a chill go down his spine. He doesn't understand why, but he's frightened. Tomorrow he will start at Davis, Morgan, and Lugner Law Offices.

CHAPTER SEVENTEEN

I barely slept all night. I am excited and frightened and sad and overjoyed all at the same time. I am also nervous. I'm still not sure that I am making the right decision. But I do know deep down that it is the only decision. I get up and get dressed in my simple, yet comfortable and not too disastrous outfit, still giggling over Joe's hospital gown from yesterday. When I am ready to walk out the door I notice a post-it note on the inside of my door. It says:

Lou, today is the day for Joe. Last job. Dangerous. – Gabby

I read the note a couple of times. Could the timing be any worse? Today is Joe's last job, which means I have to stay close, but I also have to get to Lugner's office at some point. I feel a whole host of butterflies take flight in my stomach. Today is the day for Joe. Today he finds out who Deedy really is, that he has been doing temp jobs for God. Today he gets welcomed into Heaven. Today he will reunite with loved ones. It really is a big day, and instead of being totally excited for Joe and looking forward to being there for all his discoveries, I am worried about getting into Lugner's office without having to run off and save Joe from some terrible fate.

When I get to Joe's I meet him outside. He looks a bit nervous too. I remember my last job, which was at a day care center. That was terrifying to me. Joe looks cool as a cucumber comparatively as he walks up to me and says, "Ready for some news?"

"Sure," I say, with unfelt cheerfulness. "What's up?"

"Today I start a new job!" he says.

"I heard something about that, through the grapevine. So where to this morning?"

"Davis, Morgan, and Lugner."

I look at him and probably go just a little pale. "Seriously?"

"Very. Deedy says this one is going to a big one. I figure since you have been inside, you may be able to tell me why."

"I can't think of anything, except for Suzy who is a giant bitch, but other than that…I don't know," I answer. "However, this seems like a bit of a coincidence."

"Yeah, you were just in there a couple days ago, now I'm on my way in too," Joe says casually.

"It is a bigger coincidence than that, Joe," I say. Now my nerves are showing worse than Joe's.

"Why?" he asks.

"Because I am on my way back there today. I have an appointment with," I say, leaving out the major news for right now. How would Joe react if I told him that my best friend works there and the whole reason I was watching over Joe was so that I could find that out and see her? Maybe it's better if he just doesn't know. Especially not today.

"That's great news!" Joe exclaims. "At least I will know someone there today!" He actually gets a little bounce in his step and starts to walk faster. "I'm not nearly as scared as I was!" And he actually does look a little relieved.

For a split second I stop with my obsessing of my own issue and revel just a tiny bit over the fact that I have done exactly what Deedy wanted me to do with Joe. To make him feel comfortable and safe. To give him a sense of someone having his back down here. And I had done it my own way. Not skulking around, barely hiding behind corners. I had done it by being an out in the open stalker. I laugh a bit at the thought.

However, I do wonder what could possibly happen at Davis, Morgan, and Lugner today that could be as terrifying as my experience in the day care center. Then I remember what Deedy said to me the last time I saw him, that everyone's journey is different, and that Joe is a good person. He just needs to be reminded of that. Maybe his reminder will be a bit gentler than mine had to be.

We get to Davis, Morgan, and Lugner, and we stop in front of the door. We look at one another, and I feel tears stinging behind my eyes. Joe does not realize it yet, but we have just completed the last walk to work together in Hell. I want to grab him and give him a hug and tell him that today is going to change eternity for him, but I can't. So instead I just take his hand and hold it tight and say, "Good luck, Joe."

He looks at me with a weird expression, as if to say "What is wrong with you?" but instead he says "Good luck to you too, Louise." And gives my hand a squeeze before releasing it.

We open the doors and walk through them together. I immediately scan the room for Linda but don't see her. Suzy is glaring at Joe. He introduces himself, and she dismisses him to the conference room where one of his co-workers will explain to him how to highlight the dates of meetings in every single one of their files. Ugh. Sounds like busy work to me. Also sounds so tedious that I would rather get into an Ipecac drinking contest than to have to do that all day. I do wonder if the co-worker he is about to meet is Linda, but I don't have time to sneak in there with him and check. Because Suzy bores down on me the second he is gone.

"I assume you have an appointment," she says.

"Of course I do," I say, even though I didn't exactly

make a real actual appointment. "He's expecting me." I do think that is true.

She goes back into his office and comes out. "Fine. You may go in. He will see you now." Then she turns back to her desk and keeps on doing whatever it is she does all day. My guess is eating puppies and designing houses made out of candy.

I walk casually into Lugner's office. "Hello again, Mr. Lugner," I say, kind of formally.

"Hello, Louise, I am so glad you returned. I just want you to know how very much I am looking forward to our working together," he says with his amazing smile shining brightly.

"Yes, well…about that," I say. "I don't think we will be working together."

"Excuse me?" He looks confused.

I start speaking very quickly, because I have to get it out before I lose my nerve, or my will. "I can't do it. As much as I would love to spare Linda even a moment of this pain and torment, I simply can't. Because it is not my journey. I have no right to take away her experiences for my own personal comfort or gain. And yes, she may get lost, and it may take years…but we will meet again someday, on the other side. And why should she follow me? If she does, all she will see is my back. She has to have her own chance to meet Deedy, and to have a guardian angel, and to have a last job like Joe. I can't do it. She is here because she felt she needed to be here. She has to take her own path. And if I love her, I will let her." I stop and take a deep breath. I feel so much better now that it is out.

Lugner does not seem nearly as pleased. "Are you insane?" he asks. "How can you say you love someone and leave them behind? How can you go back and tell Hank that you just arbitrarily decided that his wife needs to stay in Hell?" He actually seems a little angry at me.

Damn it, I didn't even think of Hank. He had begged me to do it. He is so new here, and he never had the experience I did with the whole temp agency thing. He will probably be pissed at me too. But hopefully, over time he will come to understand.

That is what I say now to Lugner. "And I hope you can understand too. I just feel very strongly that this is the right thing to do. And I think Linda would agree if she could." I hope and pray that she will agree someday once she knows and understands.

"You keep on telling yourself that when you are back in Paradise. Try not to think about the woman who loved you so much that she helped raise your daughter like a niece, and cried for you every single day that you were not around. Keep telling yourself that she would want you to leave her here. That everyone will understand, that you felt it was the right thing to do." I am openly sobbing now. And he stands up, which I take as a dismissal, so I also stand and head for the door. I turn around and look at him again. This man, or angel, that I thought was the most handsome specimen I had ever laid eyes on, now looks twisted and red-faced with anger. I am more than a little frightened. I decide to try to divert the subject just a little.

"I would like to say goodbye to Joe before I leave," I say through my sobs.

He presses a button and says to the air, "Suzy, bring Joe out front to say goodbye to Ms. Patterson." Then he looks at me and sneers before he adds, "Leave Linda in the conference room." That was his way of telling me that I cannot see Linda again. I choke back another sob as I leave his office and run right into Joe.

Joe looks concerned. "Louise, are you okay?" He grabs my shoulders as I start to fall.

"I think I need to sit down," I say weakly.

He takes me over to a chair and sits down next to me. "What happened?" he asks.

"Things just didn't turn out the way I thought. Lugner turned out to be kind of a jerk." "Well sure, if his name is any indication," Joe says. I suddenly remember when he told me about this office. Joe had said, "There might be thousands of Lugners down here, obviously…" What did he mean by "obviously?" And what does he mean now?

"What does his name have to do with anything?" I ask.

"My maternal grandmother was German. She was also Pentecostal. She used the word Lugner a lot. In German it translates to "Deceiver." Pretty ironic name for a lawyer, you think?" Joe answers. Then he gets a look of real concern on his face. "Louise, are you okay? You just went white, like a ghost."

I have lost all peripheral vision. There is a ringing in my ears. Deceiver. I knew he was an angel in Hell. I just didn't realize he was *the* angel of Hell. I can't breathe. I need to get out of here. I fucked up. I fucked up so badly. I must get out of here. I get up and head for the door. I am met by Suzy, the great bitch of the west. "Get out of my way!" I say to her.

"I don't think so," she replies, and she reaches out and locks the door. When she glares at me this time, her eyes shine red, like tiny embers from a fire are burning inside of her.

"I knew you were too horrible to be human!" I scream as I turn around and run straight into Joe again.

"Louise, what is happening?" Joe is now frightened too.

"Joe, I am so sorry," I plead through my fresh sobs. "But Lugner is the…" I don't have time to finish. The door to Lugner's office blows open and out he comes in all his glory. His wings unfurled and very visible to all of us.

The damned.

Because we are in his kingdom.

Satan has arrived.

Joe screams next to me, and I push him behind me. I look up at Lugner and say as bravely as I can, "Let us go, Lugner. You won't win today."

He looks at me and his eyes are filled with so much hatred. There is an overwhelming sense of malice in his voice as he practically spits his words out. "Perhaps you are right, Ms. Patterson. But I cannot allow you to leave my part of the neighborhood for a second time without getting the authentic Hell experience." Then he realizes all of my nightmares. He rains fire down on us like a summer shower. Screams are heard from all over the building, and I am pretty sure some of them were mine. People start scattering around, running up to windows and doors, beating on them, trying to break through. The heat is overwhelming now and the flames are licking at us. Lugner is now high above us, and I cannot look up to see him without going blind. Suzy is laughing as she stands at Lugner's feet. I want to punch her, to feel her face against my fist. But I can't. Joe is now unconscious from the smoke and the flames and probably the fear. I see that someone has broken through the door and people have started spilling out into the street.

I grab Joe by his collar and drag him out. "You'll be okay. I'm so sorry. You'll be okay." It's my mantra as I get him out into the street. I stand there and scream both inside my head and outside. "Gabby! Send help! Please!"

I start to scan the folks standing on the street, sitting on the curb, or lying on the sidewalk. Linda is not here. I look back at the building that used to say "Davis, Morgan, and Lugner. Now it is just a ball of fire. I put my head

144

down, scream to release the tension, and dive back into the building.

The smoke is now suffocating. The heat hits me like a wall as I run through the building looking for the conference room. I go by something that looks like it might be a kitchen, and then a restroom, and finally a conference room. It is engulfed in fire and I can barely see. I walk through feeling my skin burning and my nose is filled with the stench of burning hair. I finally see a shape in the darkness and I move closer. Linda has passed out, her poor old body splayed across the table with burning files surrounding her like candles at a vigil.

I am able to lift her. She is very light. One of the benefits to living into your 90s. I carry her outside and try to force some fresh air into her. I lean over her, sobbing and holding on to her for dear life. "I am so sorry," I say to her. "I don't want to leave you here. I don't want you to suffer." I wish that her eyes would open and she would see me. If I could explain everything maybe it would make sense to her. Maybe it would make sense to me.

There are hands on my shoulder. I look up and see Will. "Will! You are here!" I stand to grab him and hold him so tight that I think at that moment we were one person.

"Of course we are here. We wouldn't let you do this on your own," he says with so much kindness that I'm reduced to tears again.

"We?" I ask. "Who else is here?"

"Look over there," he says with a wide smile.

I look where he is pointing and see Gabby. Beautiful Gabby doing what angels are supposed to do. She is not making coffee or making sure everyone is on time. Today she is not a glorified coffee maker or alarm clock. Today she is an archangel! Suddenly I understand all the terror, but also the sheer awe that archangels inspire. Today

Gabby's wrath is unleashed, and I am more thankful than I can describe that she's doing it on my behalf. She flies over the law office and with a wave of her hand the fire goes out, then she turns to face the Devil. I see Lugner standing on the street, looking almost frightened. He waits until she lands and starts mending the wounded before he disappears. "So much for his kingdom," I say, and Will laughs.

I approach Gabby as she is hovering over Linda. "Will she be okay?" I ask nervously.

"She will be fine," Gabby says. "But she won't wake up until you are gone." She looks at me and gives me a sad smile.

"That's okay," I say with genuine gratitude. Then I ask, "Will she understand?"

Gabby looks at me and puts her arm around me. "Not today. Not tomorrow. But someday, yes. Lou, you know how this story ends. Just be patient, she will come. In her own time."

CHAPTER EIGHTEEN

Gabby picks up the unconscious Joe and carries him back to the agency. Will and I walk together without talking. When we get back, I stop at the elevator and say, "I'll be back. I have to talk to someone."

Will says, "He will be okay, Lou. Just be honest with him."

I approach Hank's door with trepidation. I knock, and he opens the door slowly. He looks at me with shock and concern. I look down at my charred clothes and soot covered skin. "It's been a bad day," I say.

"Come in!" Hank says and leads me into the living room. He gets me a cold glass of water that I drink quickly. Then I look at him and start to cry.

"What happened?" he asks, his concern etched deeply in his face.

I try to tell him the whole story. I keep having to stop when I get so upset that I can no longer form the words. When I am finally done, I look at him with pleading eyes. "Can you forgive me Hank? Can you understand?"

Hank grabs my hands and squeezes them. "Can you forgive me?" he asks through tears of his own.

"Why should I forgive you?"

"I had no idea what I was asking you to do. I don't know anything about Hell, Louise. The fact that you had to fight the devil himself...what if you had agreed? What would that have cost you? And whatever the price, it would be on my head because I asked you to do it." He sits back and searches for the right words to say. "You made the right decision. Linda has to do this, and she will do it her way. Just like you have done everything you have your own way. There is nothing to forgive, Louise.

You have always loved Linda, and you proved that when you left her exactly where she needed to be."

I hug Hank for a long time before heading back to the agency. Now that the literal smoke has cleared, I have to face Gabby. I think I am as frightened of this as I was when I realized Lugner was Satan.

I walk in, and Gabby is sitting alone in the lobby. She looks at me and gives me an appraisal with her gaze that makes me wish I could go home and change. "You are a mess, Louise," she says. "Coffee?"

"Please," I answer. I sit and wait for her to hand me the mug. I breathe in the aroma and immediately am crying once again. This is the theme for the day. Louise Patterson, the woman who never runs out of tears.

"Did I forget to put cream in it?" Gabby jokes with me.

I just launch. "Oh, Gabby. I'm so stupid! I am the biggest, most arrogant, most unbelievable dim jerk in the universe! I was conniving with the devil!" I am now wracked with sobs.

"You really are pretty arrogant if you believe that you are the only person to ever be tempted by Lugner. That is his game. He makes it sound better to do it his way. He had to trick you because he knew you were coming from a place paved with good intentions. If you wanted to openly defy Deedy he would have been completely honest with you about him or about the contract he would have made you sign. And at the end of the day, when you had to make a decision, you made the right one."

"Will Deedy be angry?" I say, like a frightened child.

"Why did you want Linda to be free from Hell?" Gabby asks.

"Because she is a good person. She was my best friend. She loved the people in her life, including my daughter. She is more than her mistakes," I say with renewed passion.

"So what you were thinking of doing came from a place of love?"

"Of course, unconditionally!" I say.

"And who is the highest example of unconditional love?" I see where she is going with this.

"Deedy," I murmur.

Just then Joe comes out of Deedy's office looking shaken but overjoyed. "Speaking of Deedy, I think Joe just got re-introduced to him," I say with a smile.

"Creator…my creator…I've been working for…Gabby! You have wings!" Joe is still a little star-struck. He looks at me and gives me a huge grin. "You have known, right? This whole time?"

"Of course I have. What kind of guardian angel would I be if I hadn't?"

"Guardian angel? I knew you didn't fix elevators!"

We are all laughing as Joe pulls out a post-it note. "Louise, I have to go to this place. It is called WF&PI. Will you be coming with me?"

"Not this time. But you will be fine. That place will rock your afterlife!" I say, giving him a congratulatory pat on the back. "And I will see you very soon." He offers me a hug, and I happily take it.

"I'll walk with you Joe," Gabby says, then whispers to me, "He has so many friends and family waiting for him, it's going to be a long night."

"I'll hang back here for a little while if that is okay?" I ask. "I just feel like being alone for a minute or two."

"Certainly. But please, do *not* make coffee. Drink what is there. If I come back and find a mess—"

"I know, I know, there will be a smiting in my future." I tease.

After they leave, I stand and look around at the sparse lobby. I choose a chair and go and kneel, putting my folded hands under my chin, and begin to speak.

"Hello, Deedy. I am not sure you can hear me. But I want to say I am sorry that I almost got sucked into a really bad idea, and for getting Linda and Joe caught in the crossfire of my bad decision-making. I'm also sorry I was kind of a crap guardian angel to Joe. I don't know how many other guardian angels ever had their charges deliberately ditch them, but I am sure it was not many. And I have to say I am sorry that I wanted to punch Suzy in the face, but that is really hard to apologize for, because she had it coming. So I guess I will just apologize for not wanting to apologize for wanting to hit her. Does that make sense? I also just want to say thank you for letting me see Linda, and for letting me get to know Joe. Damn, Deedy, I miss you. And I love you. Amen."

I get up and turn around and look out the window. It is all just bright light, blinding me. But I let it sear my vision and dry my tears. Suddenly I am startled by a strange sound. It is the sound of jingling. Like bells on Santa's sleigh…or change in a jar!

I turn and see the curse jar sitting on the chair where I was just praying. I laugh as I put a quarter in it. Then I feel someone take my hand.

I look up into the face of Deedy. The face I know with the pointy nose and the funny teeth and those huge expressive eyes. "Deedy!" I exclaim as I launch into his arms.

He wraps his arms around me and holds me close. I feel renewed and refilled. I feel whole again. My vision clears, and I can see everything. It is all back. But the most important thing that is back is Deedy. "I have never been so happy to see anyone more than I am to see you," I say with fresh tears falling. "I missed you so much."

"I missed you too, my darling girl," Deedy says in his Welsh brogue. "But I will say you did a tremendous job with Joe. Mae gwaith da!"

"I even missed your gibberish," I say giddily. "And thanks, but I know I didn't do everything right."

"So you met Lugner. What did you expect, that you can hang out in Hell and never run into him?" Deedy says casually.

"I think I made it worse for Linda instead of better. She still has to work for him."

"No, she does not. Just because she is in his territory, does not mean that she is not mine. I have already arranged for her to have another job. And I'm getting her out of that hotel room and into an apartment. She won't have it easy, but you didn't make it any harder for her."

"Thank you, Deedy! But I have to tell you something. I didn't just meet Lugner." Suddenly I feel the need to confess. "At first, well...for most of the time...I actually thought he was attractive." I wince at my own words.

"Oh, please," Deedy says dismissively "Back in the day, before the fall, when he was with us up here? Gabby and the others were nuts about him. They treated him like Elvis." He laughs.

"Thanks again," I say with more gratitude than I can ever really express. I asked for this demotion and you gave it to me. But I think you knew that you were giving me much more." I am being totally honest with him now.

He looks at me with that look of pure affection. "And I haven't even gotten started yet. Louise, I have something for you that I think you have finally earned." Then he slaps me hard on the back.

"Ouch! That hurt!" I whine at him. But then I realize that there is a new sensation where he had made contact. I feel like I have extra arms or something, but when I look to my side I see them. Not arms. Wings!

"Really?" I say overjoyed.

"Yes, really. But no powers yet. You have to work

with Gabby, and we are talking a whole new skill set, Louise." Deedy smiles down on me, and I really do feel like I can fly.

"I can. I will. Thank you. Thank you. Thank you." I am so excited.

"And that means you will be on her schedule, so you might have to get used to being a morning person," Deedy says.

"Stop trying to depress me," I murmur. "You can't make this bad. These are wings!" I am now dancing around the office.

"Then why don't you take them for a spin?" Deedy opens up the window.

I look at him once more and say, "Thank you for everything."

And then I leap and start to soar!

As I am looking down on Heaven and Hell, I am considering what I have learned.

That each of us must take our own journey. When someone decides they are taking a different path than you would take, or you would like them to take, that it is not your right to take away that choice. Understand that if you love them…you will let them. Even if that means letting them go.

We are not who we are in spite of our mistakes. Many of us are who we are because of our mistakes.

Not everyone who offers to lead you has your best interest at heart. Likewise, sometimes people who let you pull yourself out of a bad situation do.

Face all things in life first with love. When you do that, then you will always be making the right decision. Don't measure love by how much you can take. Measure love by how much you can give. That is unconditional love.

If you find someone willing to go through Hell to be

with you, never take them for granted.

And finally, it is okay to fall every once in a while. But just never forget, with enough faith and enough love, you can *fly*!

THE END

AFTERWORD

The Parable of the Little Bird…

Once there was a little bird that did not fly south for the winter. She was so happy with that decision that she sat on her branch singing a happy tune. It got so cold, the bird froze and fell to the ground in a large field. While she was lying there, a cow came by and said, "Poor little bird." Then turned around and dropped a cow pie on her. She was very surprised, but was also suddenly very warm. So she began to sing a happy tune.

A passing cat heard the bird singing and came to investigate. Following the sound, the cat discovered the bird under the pile of cow dung. "Poor little bird," the cat said and promptly dug her out, cleaned off every single feather, then opened up his mouth and ate her in one gulp!

The moral of the story is:

Not everyone who shits on you is your enemy.

Not everyone who gets you out of shit is your friend.

And when you're in deep shit, but you are warm? Sing a happy tune!

Yes, it's another Hell story. Much to my own surprise. I thought after I had written Awake In Hell that I was done with Louise. I had told her story of redemption and forgiveness, and she ended up in Heaven, so what else was left?

Turns out she had a few more lessons to learn, as did I. I am still learning to let go and allow others to take their own path. This is especially true for my children, who are just starting to dip their toes into the pool of life. However, I am also still learning from my own parents, which is kind of depressing since I am officially middle-aged and should be wise by now, right? I am also a newlywed at this age, and I am learning how to love in a lot of ways for the very first time. Congratulations to everyone who got it right from the beginning, but for me I have to say, there is something to be said for making that commitment at this stage of life. With all the experiences, the life lessons, and even the baggage that you bring to a relationship, it guarantees that you will never stop learning from one another!

So I wanted to say Thank You for coming back for more Louise, more Gabby, more Deedy, and welcoming with open arms all the new guys. I hope whatever you saw in Awake In Hell, you are also able to see in this.

I also wanted to say Thank You to everyone who has been so great to me since this journey began four years ago. I was so broken, and I wrote to heal my own heart and soul and find a path to forgiveness. But so many of you have written, sent messages on Facebook, wrote reviews on Amazon, or have come up to me to tell me in person that you were also touched in some way by these books, and for that I will always be grateful.

I sincerely hope that each and every one of you are happier today than you were yesterday. And I hope all your tomorrows are wonderful!

Thank you, and Deedy Bless!

-Helen

ABOUT THE AUTHOR

Gabrielle Mappone

Helen Downing likes to describe herself as a trophy wife, a bit of a diva, and of course Author of her own destiny! In reality, she's a chubby, middle-aged wife and mother of two who is addicted to BBC Television and social networking.

Please buy this book. It's her only chance of ever fulfilling her full potential, and possibly getting into heaven.

Like "Author Helen Downing" on Facebook!

Made in the USA
Middletown, DE
27 January 2015